Sophie
Steps Up

Also by Nancy Rue

You! A Christian Girl's Guide to Growing Up
Girl Politics
Everyone Tells Me to Be Myself ... but I Don't Know Who I Am

Sophie's World Series
Meet Sophie (Book One)
Sophie Steps Up (Book Two)
Sophie and Friends (Book Three)
Sophie's Friendship Fiasco (Book Four)
Sophie Flakes Out (Book Five)
Sophie's Drama (Book Six)

The Lucy Series
Lucy Doesn't Wear Pink (Book One)
Lucy Out of Bounds (Book Two)
Lucy's Perfect Summer (Book Three)
Lucy Finds Her Way (Book Four)

Other books in the growing Faithgirlz!™ library

Bibles
The Faithgirlz! Bible
NIV Faithgirlz! Backpack Bible

Faithgirlz! Bible Studies
Secret Power of Love
Secret Power of Joy
Secret Power of Goodness
Secret Power of Grace

Fiction

From Sadie's Sketchbook
Shades of Truth (Book One)
Flickering Hope (Book Two)
Waves of Light (Book Three)
Brilliant Hues (Book Four)

The Girls of Harbor View
Girl Power (Book One)
Take Charge (Book Two)
Raising Faith (Book Three)
Secret Admirer (Book Four)

Boarding School Mysteries
Vanished (Book One)
Betrayed (Book Two)
Burned (Book Three)
Poisoned (Book Four)

Nonfiction

Faithgirlz! Handbook
Faithgirlz Journal
Food, Faith, and Fun! Faithgirlz Cookbook
No Boys Allowed
What's a Girl to Do?
Girlz Rock
Chick Chat
Real Girls of the Bible
My Beautiful Daughter
Whatever!

Check out www.faithgirlz.com

the beauty of believing

Sophie
Steps Up

2 BOOKS IN 1
Includes *Sophie Under Pressure*
and *Sophie Steps Up*

Nancy Rue

ZONDER**kidz**

ZONDERVAN.com/
AUTHOR**TRACKER**
follow your favorite authors

ZONDERKIDZ

www.zonderkidz.com

Sophie Steps Up
ISBN 978-0310-73851-0
Copyright © 2005, 2013 by Nancy Rue

Sophie Under Pressure
Copyright © 2009 by Nancy Rue

This title is also available as a Zondervan ebook.
Visit www.zondervan.com/ebooks

Requests for information should be addressed to:
Zonderkidz, 5300 Patterson Ave. SE, Grand Rapids, Michigan 49530

Published in association with the literary agency of Alive Communications, Inc., 7680 Goddard Street, Suite 200, Colorado Springs, CO 80920. www.alivecommunucations.com

Zonderkidz is a trademark of Zondervan.

Printed in the United States

13 14 15 16 17 18 19 /DCI/ 24 23 22 21 20 19 18 17 16 15 14 13 12 11 10 9 8 7 6 5 4 3 2 1

So we fix our eyes not on what is seen,
but on what is unseen.
For what is seen is temporary,
but what is unseen is eternal.

—2 CORINTHIANS 4:18

Sophie Under Pressure

One

Sunlight hit Sophie LaCroix smack in the eyes as she and her dad stepped from the NASA building.

Solar rays, Sophie corrected herself. If she was going to make a movie about outer space, she was going to have to start thinking more scientifically.

Her dad grabbed her elbow—just before she stepped off the curb into the employees' parking lot.

"Let me at least get you to the car before you go off into La-La Land," Daddy said.

Sophie gave him her wispy smile. Not because he was right about La-La Land. Her daydreams were much more sophisticated than that. She grinned because he was grinning, instead of scolding her for not paying attention to her surroundings, the way he used to do.

"Sorry," Sophie said. "Did I almost get run over?"

"Not this time," Daddy said. He imitated her high-pitched voice, but that was okay too. His eyes were doing the good kind of teasing.

Sophie hoisted her pretty-skinny, short self up into Daddy's black Chevrolet pickup that he called the Space Mobile and whipped the light brown strands of her down-to-the-shoulders hair off her face.

I'm going to have to wear it in a braid if I'm going to play an astronaut in the movie, she thought. *You can't have a bunch of hair flying around in your space helmet.*

Did they call them helmets? Would hair actually fly around with that no-gravity thing they were talking about?

Sophie sighed as she adjusted her glasses. There was so much she was going to have to find out.

"All right, dish, Soph," Daddy said. "Your mind's going about nine hundred miles an hour."

"No, the speed of light—which is faster than anything."

Daddy arched a dark eyebrow over his sunglasses as he passed through the NASA gate. "Somebody was paying attention."

"Okay, so what does NASA stand for again?" Sophie said.

"National Aeronautics and Space Administration."

"Oh." Sophie spun that out in her head. "Then it should be NAASA."

Daddy shook his head. "That would sound like a sheep. *Naaa.*"

"What's 'aeronautics'?" She knew she could ask her best friend, Fiona, who knew what every word in life meant, but there was no time to waste. There was a film to be made.

"It's anything that has to do with making and flying aircraft," Daddy said.

Sophie decided she and the Corn Flakes would probably stick to the space part, which had real possibilities.

"Anything else you need to know for your report?" Daddy said.

"My what?"

"Your report. You know—Kids Go to Work with Dads Day. Don't you have to write up something for school?"

"Oh," Sophie said. "Yeah."

Daddy gave her a sideways glance. "Don't think I don't know what's going on in there," he said. He tapped her lightly on the forehead. "You can make your movie. Matter of fact, I WANT you to so you won't leave the planet when you're supposed to be doing your schoolwork."

Sophie nodded. The only reason he had given her the video camera was so she would spin out her dreams on film instead of letting them draw her right out the window when she was in class.

"Can I trust you to do your report as soon as you get home, without my having to check it?"

"No," Sophie said. "You better check it."

Dad chortled. That was the way Fiona always described it when Sophie's dad laughed.

Yeah, Fiona was definitely good with words. Sophie wanted to get her started writing the script right away. And Maggie would need plenty of time to work on costumes. And Kitty had to get the graphics going—

"Earth to Sophie." Daddy landed the truck in the driveway, and Sophie reentered the atmosphere.

"The report. By nineteen hundred hours."

Sophie did a quick calculation in her head. "Seven o'clock," she said.

"Roger," Daddy said.

"Over and out."

Sophie tried to keep a very scientific face as she ran into the house, headed for the stairs. If she didn't stay completely focused, nineteen hundred hours was going to come and go—and so would the video camera. "Hi, Mama, how are you?" Sophie's mom said sarcastically from the kitchen doorway. "Let me tell you about my day."

Sophie turned around, hand tight on the banister. Mama's brown-like-Sophie's eyes were shining at her, right out of the halo of her curly frosted hair. She looked impish—the way people often said Sophie herself did.

"Hi, Mama," Sophie said. She edged up another step. "I'll tell you all about it later. I have to get my report done."

"Sorry, Mama," Daddy said from behind Sophie's mom. "She has her orders."

Sophie's hand got even tighter on the banister as she watched the happy elf go back inside her mother, to be replaced by a stiff face.

"I see," she said. "You go on then, Dream Girl."

And then Mama turned back to the kitchen without even looking at Daddy.

Sophie hurried up the steps so she wouldn't have to hear the silence that was going to freeze up the whole kitchen. Every time Mama and Daddy were in the same room lately they turned into popsicles. It had been way back before Thanksgiving that she'd last heard them laugh together, and this was January. Sophie closed her bedroom door and headed for her bed—the best place for thinking in the whole entire galaxy. As soon as Daddy looked over her paper, she would have the all-clear to dream the dreams that had to come before Corn Flakes Productions—Sophie, Fiona, Kitty, and Maggie—could start on the film.

She sighed happily to herself as she pulled out her notebook, selected the blue-green gel pen—*a very aeronautical color*, she thought—and went to work.

At least it was Mr. Denton, the language arts teacher, she was writing for. He liked it when she wrote about things just the way she saw them. In blue-green words, she took him all the way through the huge telescope where you could see the craters of the moon like they were right next door — and the robotic arm they were building to capture satellites from space shuttles and work on them — and the plants that had actually been grown in space.

She polished it off with the best part: the simulated space station. She'd learned that "simulated" meant it was a fake but it was just like the real thing. She'd been allowed to go into that and see how it orbited all the time and what kind of experiments they did in there in microgravity. She hadn't even heard of microgravity before, and now she could imagine herself in it — and that was when what she was supposed to do next hit her.

I know now, Sophie wrote in her final paragraph, *that I am called to make a major film about a brave girl astronaut named—*

Sophie paused, gel pen poised over paper. She didn't quite have the name yet. Daddy would still let it pass without that one detail.

It is my responsibility to put what I have learned on film, she wrote on, *so that others may have their eyes opened* — THAT was brilliant — *to the wonderful world of outer space.*

She signed her name with a flourish and sank back into the pillows to survey her work. There were probably some words spelled wrong, she knew that. She wasn't that good of a student yet — even though she had come a way-long way since she'd started at Great Marsh Elementary back in September. Back then she had been failing, but that was before she started seeing Dr. Peter. He was her therapist, and he was a Christian like her, and he could help her with ANY problem.

Sophie sat up and cocked an ear toward her door. On the other side of it she could hear her older sister, Lacie, clamoring up the stairs with her basketball and her gym bag and her backpack full of honors classes books. In the way-far background, her five-year-old brother, Zeke, was watching SpongeBob and yelling out "SquarePants" every couple of minutes.

But other than that, the house was too quiet.

I wonder if Dr. Peter could tell me why Mama and Daddy don't seem to like each other that much anymore, Sophie thought.

But it was a cold thought she couldn't hold without feeling shivers.

Tossing her glasses aside and closing her eyes, Sophie went back to NASA in her mind, back to the space station where the girl astronaut had come into her imagination straight out of the stratosphere—the absolute highest part of the earth's atmosphere—

Stratosphere! Sophie thought. *That's her—my—last name. No, too long. How about Stratos for short?*

Perfect. After that the first name came easy. Stellar. Like the stars. No, make that Stella.

Stella Stratos. Astronaut Stella Stratos.

Astronaut Stella Stratos looked up from the complicated calculations on her computer screen to see one of her assistants standing in the doorway of the simulator.

"Can't you see I'm working?" Stella said to the clueless young woman.

"No, I can see you're going loopy again."

Sophie blinked. It was Lacie, combing out her wet, curly dark hair and giving Sophie her usual you-are-such-an-airhead look from narrowed blue eyes.

"Who are ya today?" Lacie said. Then without waiting for an answer, she said, "Come on; Mama's got dinner ready."

I wonder what they eat when they're traveling in outer space, Sophie thought as she followed Lacie downstairs. There was so much to learn.

Which was why she was ready to get the Corn Flakes right on it the next morning when they met, as always, at the swings before school when there was good weather—a way-rare thing in Virginia in January. It was perfect for thoughts of filming.

Before they were all even settled into their swings, Sophie was spilling out everything that had happened at NASA. She skimmed the soles of her boots over the slushy puddle that had formed under her swing.

"What's going on?" she said. "Y'all are looking at me weird."

"It isn't weirdness," Fiona said. "It's envy."

She cocked her head at Sophie so that one panel of golden-brown hair fell over a gray eye. Her usually creamy-coffee skin was chappy-red with the cold.

"Envy?" Sophie said. That was a stretch, seeing how Fiona was way rich and had more stuff even than the Corn Pops did. Those were the popular girls who practically wore their clothes inside out so everybody could see their labels.

Fiona tightened the hood on her North Face jacket. "I had the most boring day in life yesterday. I couldn't go to work with my dad, so I went with my mom."

"But your mom's a doctor," Kitty said. Her blue eyes were wider than they were most of the time. Everything surprised Kitty. She really was like a cat.

Fiona twitched her eyebrows. "That means she sees patients all day long—and that means I had to sit in the office with her receptionist and see her like once every twenty minutes. At lunchtime, I called my Boppa to come pick me up."

"Yeah," Maggie said. "That's boring." She spoke in her thud-voice, so that every word came out like the final say on just about anything. Sophie sometimes wondered if that was because Maggie was Cuban, and English wasn't her native language. Fiona always said it was just because Maggie was bossy.

"Mine was even boringer than yours," Kitty said. She was starting to whine, and she flipped her ponytail. She did both of those things a lot. "I didn't get to spend that much time with my dad either, since he's a pilot."

"You didn't get to go up in a plane?" Sophie said.

"She couldn't," Maggie said. "It's the Air Force. They don't let civilians fly in their planes."

"How do YOU know, Maggie?" Fiona said.

It's only 8:15 in the morning, Sophie thought, *and they're already getting on each other's nerves.*

"What about you, Maggie?" Sophie said.

Maggie shrugged. "Since I don't have a dad I went to work with my mom, but that was no big deal because I go to work with her every Saturday."

"But she does such cool stuff!" Sophie said. Maggie's mother was a tailor, and she made all the costumes for their films. Sophie thought Senora LaQuita was the most talented Cuban woman she'd ever met. Actually, she was the only Cuban woman she'd ever met.

"So you see why we have father-envy, Soph," Fiona was saying. "You had the best day of any of us."

"I bet I know what you're going to say, Sophie," Maggie said.

"No, you don't, Maggie," Fiona said. "Nobody knows what somebody else is thinking."

"She's going to say she wants to make a movie about astronauts," Maggie said.

Sophie looked at Fiona. "That WAS what I was going to say."

The bell rang, telling them they only had five minutes to get to first period. "You don't get to say anything now," Maggie said. "We have to go."

"She KNOWS that," Fiona said.

But she didn't get to say anything else, because as Sophie gave one more swing before she got out, the earth seemed to give way under her.

Actually, it was the seat of the swing, and before Sophie could even imagine herself falling through space, she was sitting—hard—in the ice-slushy puddle.

Two

Sophie was scrambling to her feet even before Kitty and Fiona could stick their hands down and haul her up. She could feel the cold muckiness on the seat of her brand-new jeans. It wasn't hard to picture the embroidered flowers on the pockets with mud caked between their petals.

"Oh, man!" she wailed. "This feels disgusting!"

"Are you okay?" Kitty said. She was whining louder than Sophie.

"I just feel gross!"

"It isn't that bad," Fiona said—without even looking at the back of Sophie's jeans.

Maggie did. She looked soberly at Sophie and said, "Yes, it is. You've got mud all the way down to your ankles. It even got on your coat."

"Enough already!" Fiona said. She glared at Maggie as she peeled off her own jacket. "Tie this around your waist and nobody will even notice 'til we get to the office."

"Yes, they will," Maggie said. "She's dripping on the ground."

"That's gonna leave a trail," Kitty put in.

"Would you two cease and desist?" Fiona said. Sophie knew she meant "Shut up!"

"Just walk tall and stare straight ahead," Fiona whispered to Sophie as she guided her through the doors into the school.

"This is so embarrassing," Sophie whispered back.

"Not if nobody sees you."

Fat chance. Of course the first people they saw were Anne-Stuart, Willoughby, B.J., and Queen Bee Julia—the Corn Pops. They were popular—which was why the Corn Flakes called them Pops—and as far as the CFs were concerned, they were pretty corny as well. When the Corn Pops had once referred to Sophie and her friends as "flakes," they adopted the name proudly. At least it made them different from THOSE girls.

THOSE girls were currently staring with their hands over their lip-glossy mouths. They didn't say anything, because they'd gotten in enough trouble for bullying the Corn Flakes before Christmas to keep them watching their backs until they went to college. Even Ms. Quelling, the social studies teacher who thought they were perfect, now kept her eye on them.

As Sophie squished toward the office, Willoughby Wiley, as usual, giggled out of control in a voice so shrill it set Sophie's nose hairs on end. Julia Cummings, who stood a head taller than all of them like an imperious monarch (Fiona's words), had her eyes slit downward in scorn for her subjects.

At her side was her handmaiden, B.J. Freeman, whose eternally red cheeks appeared to be on fire with the sheer triumph of seeing Sophie humiliated.

The only one even pretending to show sympathy was Anne-Stuart Riggins. But that was the way with Anne-Stuart, Sophie reminded herself as she sloshed past. She snorted in Sophie's direction, her powder-blue eyes watering with what was either held-back laughter or some pretty hideous allergies. Sophie wished she would sneeze her brains out right now.

"Why did THEY have to be here?" Sophie muttered to Fiona as they passed.

"They're always where you don't want them to be," Fiona muttered back. "Ignore them. They're so not worth it."

But it was almost impossible to ignore a knot of sixth-grade boys who stood just beyond the office door like they were holding up the wall. They were all wearing baggy jeans big enough for Sophie's entire family, as well as baggy T-shirts and high-tech tennis shoes, and they had short haircuts that outlined the shapes of their heads—the only thing that was different among them.

Eddie Wornom, Sophie knew, was the one with the big ol' square head over his bruiser of a body. He was clapping like an ape. Sophie expected a swearword to slip out of his mouth any minute, which always happened when he was excited.

The one with the long head was Colton Messik. His ears stuck out like open car doors, and he was always pretending he was shooting a basketball. Right now he was too hysterical for that.

And then there was the third kid, Tod Ravelli. He was like a male version of Julia, except he was short and had a head that came to a point in the front like he was from Whoville. Sophie always thought he could have been a model for one of Dr. Seuss's books.

But there was nothing funny about him in Sophie's world. He was looking at her now like she had dared crawl across his path in her state of degradation (Fiona again). "Who dragged you in?" he said.

"I did," Fiona said. "You got a problem with that?"

"Yeah," Eddie chimed in. "I smell something. Ooh—she pooped her pants!"

"No she didn't, stupid," Maggie said. "That's mud."

Eddie and Colton looked at each other and sniffed.

"No," Colton said. "That's poop."

Then they collapsed into each other, while Tod continued to stare at Sophie as if he could make her disappear.

She wished she would.

Fiona was about to shove Sophie into the office when Tod said, "Dude, just don't get any of that on me."

Fiona looked at Sophie with a familiar gleam in her eyes—a gleam Sophie could read.

"One," Sophie whispered to her.

"Two," Fiona whispered back.

"Three!" they said together.

And then Fiona whipped the jacket from around Sophie's waist and stepped back—and Sophie shook like a wet dog.

Big drops of mud, slush, and general playground filth flew off Sophie and into the air like dirty confetti. Most of it landed on Tod, speckling him in drooly brown. What didn't get on him found its resting place on Colton and Eddie. Somewhere between "One" and "Two," Maggie and Kitty had known enough to dive behind a trash can.

Shouts of "Man!", "Dude!", and "Sick!" came out of the now mud-caked trio, along with a few words from Eddie that Sophie knew she wouldn't be repeating when she told this story to Mama. While the boys were frantically de-grossing, Fiona, Sophie, Maggie, and Kitty dived into the office and shut the door behind them.

"Score," Fiona whispered.

Even Maggie agreed.

While the school secretary called Sophie's mom to bring dry clothes, Maggie gave Sophie another once-over.

"I can tell you how to get those stains out," she said.

"Just don't share that information with that bunch of Fruit Loops," Fiona said.

Kitty giggled. "Fruit Loops!"

"That's what they are." Fiona wiggled her eyebrows. "But they're SO obvious. We can handle them."

When they left the office, Sophie could hear Kitty whining all the way down the hall, "What if I don't WANT to 'handle them'?"

Sophie couldn't wait to describe the whole thing to Mama when she got there. Mama was sure to love this little tale.

But when Mama arrived, Sophie felt the story shrivel up on her lips. Mama's eyes were red and puffy—like she'd been crying. And not the sweet way Mama had of bawling over the lopsided craft projects Sophie and Lacie and Zeke had brought home to her over the years. This looked like serious crying that Mama was trying to hide under makeup she hardly ever wore.

"What's wrong, Mama?" Sophie said.

Mama gave a watery smile as she handed over a whole different outfit, down to Sophie's favorite toe socks with the frogs on them.

"I think I'm just coming down with a cold," she said.

But Sophie had seen watery-eyed colds on Anne-Stuart. This was a whole other thing.

"Do you need a hug?" Sophie said.

Mama enfolded her in her arms, shuddered a little, and then pulled away and headed straight for the door, waving over her shoulder. But Sophie had seen the tears already splashing onto her cheeks.

Sophie had a blur over her own eyes as she sat on the bathroom floor and fed her toes into the socks. *This doesn't feel good at all. What could possibly be this wrong?*

She couldn't shake it off the way she'd gotten rid of the mud. As she wriggled into fresh jeans, she thought about Dr. Peter. She only got to talk to him alone every other week now.

Next week I'm going to ask him what to do, she thought.

Only—next week was a whole long way away. The chill that shivered her insides could freeze her solid in seven days. In three days. Maybe in one.

Astronaut Stella Stratos pulled the regulation NASA turtleneck sweater over her head and straightened her shoulders. This was serious family business, but she couldn't let it distract her from the work at hand. There was a movie to be made about a creation that could save the world. Somehow. She had not yet figured that part out.

Sophie knew that if she kept her mind on Stella, she'd find the way to rescue the planet. AND keep the cold thought of Mama crying away in some dark place, where it couldn't hurt so much.

Three

The Fruit Loops spent the rest of the day making disgusting noises with their armpits and sniffing the air around Sophie.

Colton picked the caked-on mud off his shoes and stuck it on Sophie's binder. Eddie dumped an entire handful of it into her backpack, and during lunch all three of them made such a big deal out of telling people to watch out because she had run out of Pampers, Sophie stuffed her peanut butter and jelly sandwich back into her lunch box with only one bite taken out of it.

"Don't let them get to you," Fiona said. "They're just imbeciles."

"What's an 'imbecile'?" Kitty said.

"Idiot," Maggie told her. "Them."

She nodded toward the three boys, two of whom were pulling a chair out from under Eddie and making a splatting noise with their very big mouths when he hit the floor.

"That's you falling out of the swing," Maggie said to Sophie.

"Duh," Fiona said.

"I'm just wondering how they knew the swing broke under me." Sophie blinked at the Corn Flakes. "We were the only ones left on the playground when it happened."

"I know how."

Sophie looked down the cafeteria table at Harley Hunter. She was an into-every-sport girl, only as far as Sophie was concerned she wasn't stuck-up like Lacie. She and her friends Gill, Nikki, and Vette—the Wheaties—sat at the Corn Flakes' lunch table most days and never made fun of them.

"How?" Kitty said to Harley.

"Because we heard those boys talking at P.E. yesterday."

"They had it planned," Gill said. "They were going to do something to the swing because they knew y'all sit there every morning."

"Hello!" Fiona said. Her gray eyes were practically popping out. "Why didn't you tell us?"

"They're morons," Harley said.

"Imbeciles," Kitty said.

"Whatever. The way they were laughing about it, we thought they were just messing around."

"We didn't think they had enough brains to know how to set up a swing to break," Gill said.

Maggie scraped back her chair. "I'm telling."

"NO!" said all the Wheaties.

Kitty's whine echoed them.

"You're probably right," Fiona said. "You tell on them, and the next thing you know, all of you are in a mud puddle. Or worse."

Maggie was looking hard at Sophie, who squirmed in her seat.

"Okay," Sophie said. "But we can't let them get away with bullying. We made a pact."

"What's a 'pact' again?" Kitty said.

Sometimes it seemed like Kitty must have failed all her vocabulary tests since second grade.

"It was our promise that we made," Sophie said patiently. "We can't let mean people get away with stuff just because we're afraid of them."

"But I can't afford to get in trouble," Harley said. "Or I won't be allowed to play basketball."

"I still think I should tell," Maggie said.

Fiona was giving Sophie the best friend's I'll-do-whatever-you-think-we-oughta-do look.

"Don't tell yet," Sophie said to Maggie. "Like Fiona said before, I bet we can handle those imbeciles ourselves."

Gill put up a hand. It took Sophie a good five seconds to realize Gill wanted to high-five.

"You're tough," Gill said to her. "I dig that."

Actually, sitting in the middle of seven girls who were all way bigger than she was, Sophie had never felt wimpier in her life. But she closed her eyes and imagined Jesus—just the way Dr. Peter had taught her to.

As usual, she didn't imagine Jesus saying anything. Dr. Peter said that would be like making up God. But it felt good to know he was just a thought away.

Help me to do the no-bully thing, please, she asked him. *Please don't let me be the wimp the Fruit Loops think I am.*

Something else made her wonder, though, as she suffered through P.E. with the Fruit Loops splashing in every puddle within three feet of her, and through math class where they delivered fake dry cleaning bills to her desk.

Why, she thought, *are the Fruit Loops all of a sudden trying to get to me? I never did anything to them. I hardly even noticed them that much until yesterday.*

I don't even LIKE boys.

As she tried to settle into last-period science class, Sophie went back to the promise she'd made—the Flakes would "handle" the Fruit Loops.

"How we will do that," Astronaut Stella said to her crew, *"I have not yet determined. But never fear. Science will be victorious."*

Sophie was still enjoying the view from the space capsule when Fiona coughed at her. That was the signal that Sophie was about to miss something important in class. Like an assignment.

Sophie focused on Mrs. Utley, whose many chins were wobbling as she passed out blue sheets of paper to the class with her pretty, plump hands. The Corn Pops called her Mrs. Fatley behind her back, but Sophie thought there was just more of her to be beautiful than most people.

"This will explain what I want in your science project," Mrs. Utley was saying. As she passed Colton's desk, he gave her a teacher's-pet grin, and then behind her back blew up his cheeks with air at Eddie, who nearly fell out of his desk.

Like he has room to laugh at her, Sophie thought. *Pig Boy.*

"I'd like for you to work in groups," Mrs. Utley went on.

The Corn Flakes all looked at one another. The Wheaties high-fived one another, and every Corn Pop grabbed onto another Corn Pop's arm like Mrs. Utley was going to dare to try to pry them apart.

Tod just gave the other Fruit Loops a nod like their working together was a done deal.

"Let's cut a frog up!" Eddie said.

"Sick, man," Colton said back.

"Yeah—that's what I'm sayin'."

"Dude, I'll puke."

"Wimp."

"Loser."

"MAJOR loser."

"I have a scathingly brilliant idea!" Fiona said to the Corn Flakes.

"Is 'scathingly' a good thing?" Kitty said.

"It is when it tells us what to do for our project." Fiona grinned at Sophie, wiggling her eyebrows at light speed. "Actually, you told us. You're the one who went to NASA. You're the one whose father is a rocket scientist. It only makes sense—we build a space station." She gave the eyebrows a final wiggle. "And I know the perfect place to do it."

"Where?" Maggie said.

"My place. Tree house. I'm the only one in the family that's allowed to go up in it. Except Boppa, of course."

Sophie loved the image of Fiona's amazing grandfather up in the tree house, bald head gleaming in the sun, hammering away at anything Fiona asked him to.

"Not only will we build a space station—" Sophie said.

"Let me guess," Maggie said. "We'll film the whole thing and have costumes and play like we're astronauts."

"Do you have a problem with that?" Fiona said to her.

Maggie shook her head. Kitty was dimpling all over.

"I'll need your plan by Wednesday," Mrs. Utley was saying. "And those of you who are in the GATE program, keep in mind that you will need to do more of the work than the other people in your groups."

For once, that wasn't a problem for Sophie. She had just gotten into the Gifted and Talented Education program—with Fiona—right before Christmas, and so far she'd felt like somebody had made a mistake putting her there. But this? This was her life every day.

Fiona whipped open the purple Treasures Book that she always carried around for the Corn Flakes, and Maggie handed her a fresh pencil with a very sharp point and a no-mistakes-yet eraser. "Start dictating, Soph," she said.

Sophie sighed happily and let Astronaut Stella Stratos take her rightful place at the podium. The plan to save the planet began.

Four

❀ 🕊 ✽

Sophie would have asked Mama's permission to go over to Fiona's the next day the minute she got home from school, but Mama was dealing with Lacie, who was having a boy crisis. Sophie was more sure than ever that males weren't worth the time it took to learn their names.

After that it was kind of funky at the dinner table. Lacie was brooding over Mr. Boy and picking at her pot roast. Mama and Daddy were talking like the people on the news—all polite with stiff laughter at things that weren't that funny. And Zeke dumped his milk over, crawled under the table three times to get his napkin, and once nibbled at Lacie's calf while he was under there.

Right after dinner, Mama left for a meeting at church, and Sophie paced her bedroom floor, the way she was sure Astronaut Stella would do when she was faced with a delay on a project. Fiona was probably that very minute searching the Internet, while Maggie and her mother were drawing pictures of costumes and Kitty was thinking of an astronaut name for herself. Sophie had learned that she had to give Kitty plenty of time to come up with these things. Her imagination muscle was still a little weak.

Mama wasn't home at bedtime, so Sophie padded out of her room in her pajamas-with-the-feet-in-them to go ask Daddy for permission. Lacie was coming back from the phone with wet eyelashes when Sophie passed her in the upstairs hall.

"Why are you wearing those?" Lacie said, pointing to Sophie's floppy feet. "You look like you're two years old."

Sophie didn't point out that it was the closest thing she had to a space suit right now. She'd learned not to share that kind of information with Lacie. Instead, she said, "Have you been crying?"

"Yes," Lacie said. Her voice got thick. "Take a little advice from me, Soph. Don't ever get a crush on a guy who turns out to be a two-faced, coldhearted little—"

"Imbecile," Sophie said.

Lacie's eyebrows shot up. "Yeah. That's the perfect word."

Sophie took a deep breath. "Mama's been crying a lot lately too," she said. "Do you think she thinks Daddy is a two-timing, cold-hearted little imbecile? Well, big imbecile."

"No, I do NOT!" Lacie said. "She and Daddy are good together!"

"Oh," Sophie said. "Then how come they hardly talk to each other anymore?"

"They DO." Lacie set her face so firmly that even her freckles seemed to stand at attention. "You just don't hear them."

"Do you hear them?" Sophie said.

"No. I don't go spying on them."

"Then how do you know?"

Sophie knew she was starting to sound like Maggie, but she couldn't stop herself.

Lacie gave her an annoyed look. "I just know," she said.

Rolling her arms up into the old T-shirt of Daddy's she was wearing, Lacie flounced to her room.

She's scared too, Sophie thought. *That scares ME.*

But Daddy himself didn't seem scared when Sophie found him, bending his big handsome head toward his computer screen, cup of coffee at his side. Sophie knew it was decaf. He and Mama usually had their mugs of it together at night.

"What's up, Soph?" he said. He glanced at her and drew his eyebrows in over his nose. "Nice outfit. I wish your mother had a pair of those. She has the coldest feet when she goes to bed, and she puts them right on *me*."

Mama and Daddy touching feet was good, Sophie decided. Although, she couldn't imagine touching some guy's feet. The image of Eddie Wornom coming after her with his huge clod-hoppers made her nauseous.

"You okay?" Daddy said.

"Yes, sir. I just wanted to ask Mama if I could go to Fiona's after school tomorrow."

Daddy took a slurp of his coffee and squinted his eyes like it was hot. Sophie could never figure out why grown-ups couldn't just wait until it cooled off a little bit.

"I don't see why not," he said. "I'll tell your mom."

"When's she coming home?"

He stopped in mid-gulp. "I can speak for her," he said. "It's fine."

There was something pointy in his voice, like she'd just told him he wasn't the boss of her.

She got on tiptoes to kiss his cheek. "I was just asking," she said. "Lacie's crying again."

Daddy's eyes suddenly got round. "The boy thing?" he said. Sophie nodded.

"Now THAT I'll leave for Mama to handle."

On her way up the stairs Sophie wondered why Daddy couldn't explain boys to Lacie. After all, he was a boy once.

It was sunny again the next day and not even cold enough for gloves. That meant it would be even warmer when she and the Corn Flakes climbed up into the tree house that afternoon. Sophie was almost too excited to eat her Cream of Wheat, and she considered feeding it to Zeke, who was crawling around under the snack bar.

"Did Daddy tell you I'm going to Fiona's after school?" she said.

Mama's hand tightened on the knife she was using to spread peanut butter. "Yes, he did. I wish you had talked to me first. I have an appointment with Dr. Peter today and I was counting on you watching Zeke for me in the waiting room."

The Cream of Wheat turned into a lump in Sophie's throat. "You mean I can't go to Fiona's?"

Mama put a top on the sandwich like she was slamming a door. "Maybe I can get Boppa to watch Zeke over there. I just don't like to take advantage of him."

"He won't mind!" Sophie said.

Mama dropped the sandwich into Sophie's lunch box and snapped it just a little too hard. "I said I'll ask him. Zeke, PLEASE get up in your chair. I don't have time for this today."

It seemed to Sophie that Mama had as much time as she always did in the morning. She told herself Mama must have gotten home late and she was cranky because she didn't get enough sleep. Now Sophie was a little cranky herself. If she didn't get to go to Fiona's, their group was going to start off their project already behind.

"Boppa will watch Zeke—you know he will," Fiona said when Sophie told her the news later on the playground.

The Corn Flakes were all gathered at the end of the slide. Even though somebody had fixed the swing, they weren't taking any chances.

"He's better behaved than our two brats," Fiona said.

Sophie had to nod. Fiona's four-year-old sister, Isabella, and her six-year-old brother, Rory, went through a new nanny about every three months. The last one, Marissa, had left after Rory snuck miniature LEGOs into her quesadilla and she broke a tooth.

"If you can't come," Maggie said to Sophie, "we'll just have to start without you."

"We will NOT start without our captain." Fiona saluted Sophie.

"How come she's the captain?" Maggie said.

"I like it when Sophie's captain," Kitty said. "She's nice."

"And she has the camera and the resources," Fiona said. "It's most advantageous for us to make her captain."

"What's 'advantageous'?" all three of them said.

Fiona looked straight at Maggie. "It means it doesn't make sense for us to do it any other way. Besides, Boppa will take care of Z-Boy and Sophie will be there and we'll go on like we planned."

"I'm bringing Tang for us to drink," Kitty said. "My father told me they drink that in outer space."

Sophie was impressed.

Mama did pick Sophie up that afternoon with Zeke in the car and dropped them both off at Fiona's.

"Don't worry, Lynda," Boppa said to Sophie's mom as Zeke bolted across Fiona's yard toward Isabella and Rory. "I won't let them hurt him."

He smiled at Mama, but his dark caterpillar eyebrows drooped, and his forehead wrinkled halfway up his shiny head. It didn't make Sophie feel any better that Boppa seemed worried about Mama too.

By the time Fiona came out to meet Sophie, flanked by Kitty and Maggie, Rory and Isabella were already screaming

35

and chasing Zeke in and out of the line of cedar trees that bordered Fiona's huge lawn, which actually had water splashing deliciously over a stone wall and a little bridge that crossed the pond the waterfall made. So many filming possibilities—

But today Sophie was much more interested in the tree house.

It was built off three big pine trees so that it was a triangle, and the only way to get to it was on a ladder that went absolutely straight up through a narrow opening in the tree house floor. Even tiny Sophie had to scrunch her shoulders together to slide through.

As the Corn Flakes climbed, a lady stood at the bottom, tucking a big jar of a very orange-looking liquid, some plastic cups, and individual bags of pretzels into a basket that was attached to a rope on a crank handle. Sophie knew that was for transporting stuff up to the tree house. She'd been up there several times before—just not for business this important.

Sophie leaned over the railing to watch her. The lady had perfectly curled hair down to her shoulders and teeth as white as Tic Tacs.

"Is she part of our ground crew?" Sophie whispered to Fiona.

"She can be," Fiona said. "Actually, she's the new nanny. Her name's Kateesha."

"She doesn't look like she has any bruises yet," Maggie said.

Kitty stroked her own hair dreamily. "She looks like Halle Berry. I wish I looked like that."

Maggie shook her head. "You'll never look like that. You're Caucasian."

"But you're just as pretty," Sophie put in quickly. It wouldn't be good to start off with Kitty in tears.

Boppa had built lockers against the railings that had lids on hinges so the girls could put stuff in them, and Sophie put her backpack in hers. She was already pretending it was a spaceship compartment. The basket arrived through the ladder hole and Fiona said, "We should eat first. We're going to need sustenance if we want our minds to be sharp."

"Define 'sustenance,'" Kitty said.

"Food," Maggie told her. "I don't know why she couldn't just say that."

"Because 'sustenance' sounds more scientific," Fiona said.

Sophie was already pouring the orange stuff into cups. A few grainy things floated to the top of each one.

"What is it?" Maggie said as she stared into hers.

"It's the Tang I was telling you about," Kitty said proudly. "It comes in this powder stuff and you mix it with water."

"Somebody didn't mix it up enough," Maggie said.

Fiona drained hers and pulled the Treasures Book out from under her arm. "Captain," she said to Sophie, "do I have your permission to present information?"

"Yes," Sophie said. "But please call me Stella. Stella Stratos."

"I haven't thought of a name yet," Kitty said. Her voice was starting to wind up.

"That can wait," Fiona said.

"I thought Sophie was captain," Maggie said.

Sophie pointed at the book. "Let's see your information."

It would be advantageous for us to get this going, Stella thought, *or I'm going to have a mutiny on my hands.*

Fiona produced some pages that she had printed off the Internet. Like about twenty. Fiona never did anything halfway.

"Your report please, crew member," Sophie said to her.

Fiona cleared her throat, very scientifically, Sophie thought—and pointed to a paragraph. "We would actually be called an expedition crew. We're building an international space station that will weigh a million pounds when it's done and there'll be six laboratories in it for research."

"Do the stations have names?" Sophie said.

Fiona frowned importantly over the page. "One's Destiny. They call one Leonardo."

Kitty squealed. "Let's call ours that!"

"We're going to need to get to know the station before we name it," Sophie said.

"Like a puppy?" Maggie said.

"Is this a picture of it?" Sophie pointed to a long narrow shiny vehicle that had two enormous flat wings above it and so many robot-like arms she expected it to come alive right on the page. Her heart actually started to race. Yeah, this had more dreaming tucked into it than anything she had ever thought up before.

"We're gonna build that?" Maggie said. She pulled her chin back into her neck.

"Something like it," Sophie said.

"That's so cool," Kitty said. "I want to work this thing." She poked a finger at the robotic arm that hung down like a big metal sea serpent.

"What does it do?" Maggie said.

"I don't know," Kitty said. "I just think it's cute."

"Science can't be cute," Fiona said. "It can be fascinating, and it can be exciting, and it can be scintillating—"

"I'll go with exciting," Kitty said.

Sophie crawled over to her box again. "I'm gonna get the camera and take some before pictures."

"We should think of what we're trying to prove for our project," Maggie said. "I mean ..." She wagged her head a little. "Shouldn't we, Captain? Mrs. Utley said we have to put that in our plan, and it's due tomorrow."

"That's true," Fiona said. She looked to Sophie like she would rather have admitted she had rabies than agree with Maggie.

"I trust you all to do that while I film," Sophie said.

Fiona, Kitty, and Maggie bent their heads over Fiona's pages, and she explained the basics of what a space station did. Sophie filmed the storage boxes, the railing, and the hole for the ladder that had its own hinged door that had to be kept closed when they were up there so that nobody would accidentally fall through—Boppa's rule.

As she captured the tree house with her camera, Sophie had to admit that it was pretty cool just as it was. It was like being on top of the planet, above even the grown-up world.

I just want to lie on my back and look up, Sophie thought. She imagined closing her eyes and dreaming up Captain Stella Stratos for hours on end.

"Are you filming with your eyes closed?" Maggie said.

Sophie popped her eyes open. Oh, yeah. The before movie. No matter how much she loved this tree house as it was, it was soon going to be transformed.

"We have agreed on an experiment, Captain," Fiona said.

"We didn't vote on it," Maggie said.

"So we'll vote already," Fiona said between clenched teeth. "Who wants to make building the space station the experiment, and we tell how it's different from building it in outer space?"

She, Kitty, and Maggie all raised their hands.

"Why did we just do that?" Fiona said.

Sophie gave a hurried nod. "Then it's decided. Now I want to film each of you stating your name and what your job is."

Of course, Sophie had to turn off the camera immediately and help everybody figure out a name and a job, and make sure Fiona didn't get sick of Maggie and haul off and smack her. If that happened, there would be more screaming than they were hearing from down below. It sounded like somebody had somebody tied up. Sophie was afraid to look. She hoped it wasn't that pretty Kateesha lady.

It was decided that Sophie definitely would be Captain Stella Stratos, the head of the space station. Maggie pointed out that Fiona actually knew more about space stations than Sophie did, but Kitty and Fiona overruled her.

Fiona was to be called Jupiter. She was in charge of the experiment itself. Maggie couldn't argue with that, since she'd already said Fiona was better for the job. Besides, Fiona needed to do more because of GATE.

The name they gave Kitty was Luna, after the moon. She kept repeating it like she was afraid she would forget it. Fiona said Kitty should be her assistant.

By the time they got to Maggie, she had picked out her own name: Nimbus. She told them it was a type of cloud.

"I know," Fiona said. "A very DARK cloud."

Kitty nodded. "She does have black hair. I wish I had hair like yours, Maggie."

Maggie looked all around the tree house like she didn't know where to put a compliment.

"I think I should keep all the records of the results of the experiment," Maggie said finally. "I'm the only one of us who's really good at that."

"Hello! Rude!" Fiona said.

"Who always gets hundreds in spelling and handwriting?"

"I get ninety-seven's."

"So I'm better at it than you."

"You're the record keeper, Nimbus," Sophie said. She was suddenly so tired, she wanted to crawl into her wooden box. Or maybe put Maggie in hers.

Captain Stella Stratos knew she was going to have to figure out how to handle crew members who always acted like they wanted to throw each other into the ozone layer.

Just then the loudest scream yet pierced the air from the ground right up to the space station. The Corn Flakes all scrambled to the railing, just in time to see Zeke flying off the deck, frantically flapping his little arms, which were clad in a pair of flowered pillowcases. As Sophie watched in horror, her little brother hit the ground like a crashing plane, pillowcases crumpled on either side.

And then he just stayed there, and he didn't move at all.

Five

By the time Sophie got to Zeke, Boppa and Kateesha were already there. Isabella and Rory were nowhere in sight.

"Is he dead?" Sophie said. She slid in on her knees and peered, terrified, at Zeke.

"No, he's not dead," Kateesha said. "But I know two other kids who are going to be when I get a hold of them."

"You go take care of them," Boppa said to her. "Just try not to break any bones."

Kateesha hurried off, and Zeke started to cry. That definitely meant he wasn't dead.

"Where do you hurt, little buddy?" Boppa said.

"Everywhere!" Zeke wailed.

"Is his whole body broken?" Sophie said. "Should we call nine-one-one?"

"Let's take a look here," Boppa said. His voice was as soft and calm as always.

He went over Zeke limb by limb. Everything seemed to be in working order. The ice-cream sandwich Kateesha brought him and the apologies from Isabella and Rory got him smiling again. Personally, Sophie didn't think he should forgive those two little monsters. They didn't seem all that sincere to her.

"Why did you jump off the deck in the first place?" Mama asked Zeke later on the way home.

"I didn't jump," Zeke said. "Izzy and Rory pushed me."

"Why did they push you?"

"They wanted to see if I could fly with those wings we made."

Mama glanced at him in the rearview mirror. "Let me tell you something, Z," she said. "You cannot fly. Period. So don't try it again."

"Sophie and them's gonna fly," he said. His bee sting of a mouth was going into a pout.

"No, we're not!" Sophie said. "We're just building a space station."

Mama lowered her voice and leaned a little toward Sophie. "Just to be on the safe side, don't ever take him up into that tree house."

Sophie gave her a somber nod. And then she let out a long breath of relieved air. At least Mama didn't say Sophie couldn't go over to Fiona's and take Zeke from then on. From the serious way she'd seen Mama talking to Boppa before they started for home, Sophie suspected Mama was going to have more sessions with Dr. Peter.

For the next week, the astronauts worked every minute they had setting up the space station. They decided to call it *Freedom 4*. "Freedom" because it was going to save the world, although Captain Stella Stratos hadn't yet figured out how that was going to work. And "Four" sounded the best with "Freedom." When they got to the space station the day after they named it, there was a painted sign up there that read, "Welcome to

Freedom 4," and all the names on the boxes had been switched to the girls' astronaut names.

Boppa was doing a lot to help them, but they were being very careful to do most of the work themselves with Boppa just overseeing. Mrs. Utley said nobody was allowed to have their parents do their science projects for them.

"These are going to go on display in the science fair for the PTO meeting next month," she told the class. Her chins were really wiggling, so Sophie knew she meant business. "But if any group turns in a project that was obviously done by an adult, it will not be shown. Period."

Sophie heard the Corn Pops whispering to one another like startled bees. As for the Fruit Loops—they were all leaning back in their chairs with their arms folded over their chests. *They think they could get away with having a brain surgeon do their whole project*, Sophie thought. She wondered how many poor frogs they had tortured already.

"How are we going to get all this into the cafeteria to put on display?" Maggie said that afternoon when they were up in the space station.

Sophie looked around at all they'd done so far—the "robot arm" they'd made from an umbrella handle and attached to the basket crank so they could move it up and down; the sets of old headphones from Kitty's dad on hooks for the astronauts; the big flat wings that hung above them that Boppa had helped them make from sheets of metal off a torn-down shed. Captain Stella had to admit that Nimbus had a point.

"Simple," Fiona said. "We'll get Mrs. Utley to set up a DVD player and a TV to show our film, and we'll find some really cool way to display our results. You know, a graph or something. That's your job, Nimbus."

Maggie frowned. "But I need information about that microgravity thing where everything floats around up in space,

so I'll know how this is different. That's your job, Jupiter."
Maggie's voice then gave its final thud: "Are you two doing
any work at all?"

She pointed a stern finger at Kitty and Fiona. Kitty shrank
back like she'd been hit with a large stick. Fiona's nostrils flared.

Uh-oh, Sophie thought. *Here it comes.*

"And what about you?" Fiona said. "I don't see any costumes yet. Hello!"

It wasn't the first time Fiona had gotten furious with
Maggie since they'd started working on the space station. And
Sophie really couldn't blame her. Maggie was getting bossier
by the second, and even though sometimes she was right,
Kitty whined to Sophie privately that she didn't have to be so
mean about it.

"I got enough of that when I was a Corn Pop," she told
Sophie. "I thought being a Corn Flake meant you were nice
to people."

When Maggie wasn't around, Fiona was all for voting her off
the crew, but Sophie said no. For one thing, how was Maggie
supposed to get a science project done if they kicked her out of
the group? Mrs. Utley's chins would wiggle right off her face.

"Besides," Sophie told Fiona the next morning at school
before Maggie got there, "we're Corn Flakes. We're supposed
to help people."

"We're supposed to keep them from being bullied," Fiona
said. "I feel like Nimbus is bullying us."

Sophie had noticed that Fiona always referred to Maggie
as Nimbus now. She seemed to like the way she could curl her
upper lip when she said it. Maggie definitely wasn't bringing
out the best in Fiona.

"I'll talk to her," Sophie said. "That's my job as captain."

"Good," Fiona said. "Here she comes. You can start right
now."

Fiona tested a swing and then sat down on it, arms folded. Sophie moved away from her a little and stopped Maggie before she could get too close.

"Hi, Mags," Sophie said.

"You should make up your mind what you want to call me," Maggie said. "Sometimes I'm Nimbus. Sometimes I'm Maggie. Now I'm Mags."

"Giving somebody nicknames means you like them," Sophie said.

"Oh," Maggie said. "My mother just calls me Margarita."

Sophie felt her eyes getting big. "Your real name is Margarita?"

"Yes, like the drink. And don't tell anybody at this school, or I'll be laughed at every minute."

Sophie made an X mark on her chest with her hand. "I would never do that. No Corn Flake would ever do that."

"You guys are always nice," Maggie said.

"You're a Corn Flake too, remember." Sophie sucked in some air. "And, Mags, sometimes you aren't all that nice to certain people in the group."

Maggie's eyes darted in Fiona's direction. "Did SHE tell you that?"

"She didn't have to," Sophie said. "I can see it for myself."

"She isn't the nicest person in the whole world either." Maggie's words were now firing out like bullets.

"What does THAT mean?" Fiona said. The swing was now swaying crazily where she'd lurched out of it.

"It means you've been talking trash about me to Sophie," Maggie said.

Fiona stopped just inches from Maggie's face. Sophie tried to wedge her way between them.

"I never said anything to Sophie that wasn't true," Fiona said.

Fiona's nostrils were flaring so wide, Sophie figured Mama could drive their old Suburban through one of them.

"Why didn't you just say it to me?" Maggie said.

"Okay," Fiona said. "I'll say it straight to your face!"

"Say it, then," Maggie said.

"Okay." Fiona narrowed her eyes at Maggie. "I think you are the bossiest person on the face of the earth. You act like you're the president of the United States or somebody! Always telling Kitty and me what to do—"

"Do not," Maggie said.

"Do too," Fiona said.

"Do NOT!"

"Do TOO!"

"STOP!" Sophie cried.

"No—let 'em go for it!"

That came from Colton Messik, who was suddenly standing three feet from them with the other two Fruit Loops.

"Fight!" Eddie shouted, face red. "Fight!"

Maggie turned on them like she was going to throw a punch. Sophie jumped on her back. Fiona got in front of them both and put up her hands.

"There isn't gonna be a fight, morons!" she said. "Go crawl back under your rock."

"She's dissin' you, man," Colton said to Tod. "You gonna let her get away with that?"

"She won't get away with it," Tod said. He turned like a basketball player doing a pivot, snapped his fingers in the air, and sauntered off toward the building with Colton and Eddie trailing him.

Colton walked backward and called to the Corn Flakes, "You heard him. He isn't kidding."

"Yeah, yeah," Fiona shouted back to him.

"Imbeciles," Maggie said.

"Definitely," Fiona said.

Sophie let all the air go out of her. At least they agreed on something. And for the moment, they seemed to have forgotten what it was they'd been about to fight about.

"So is it true you guys tried to kill each other in the hall this morning?" Harley said at the lunch table.

"Right in front of the office?" Gill said.

Nikki and Vette looked like they were totally convinced that it was the gospel truth and were prepared to take flight at the first sign of face scratching and hair pulling.

"It was out on the playground," Maggie said.

"Then you DID get in a fight?" Harley said.

"No, we almost did," Fiona said. She glared at Maggie.

Sophie groaned inside. So much for them forgetting why they were mad at each other.

Kitty smothered a gasp with her hand.

"What?" Fiona said. "Why are you freaking out?"

Kitty pointed toward the Corn Pops' table.

The Fruit Loops were sitting with them, talking and waving their arms all around like they were running for office.

No boys ever sat with girls. But the Fruit Loops looked like they were right at home.

Why not? Sophie thought. *They're all rich and popular and mean.*

Still, with the seven of them teaming up, it couldn't be good.

It couldn't be good at all.

That night after Zeke was tucked in, Mama went out to her Loom Room over the garage. When Sophie went downstairs to check out the flight food in the space kitchen, Daddy was

48

in front of his computer again. Sophie wondered what could possibly be so interesting on there for hours on end.

When she came out of the kitchen with a neat stack of Mama's double-fudge brownies and a glass of milk, Daddy called from his study, "Hey, Soph. What are you up to?"

"Just having a little snack," Sophie said. She headed for the stairs.

"Come in here a minute."

Sophie turned reluctantly toward the study. Maybe she shouldn't have helped herself to quite so many brownies.

Daddy took one look at her plate and said, "A little snack? Were you planning to share that with Lacie?"

"No," Sophie said.

Daddy grinned. "I love that honesty. Lacie wouldn't eat those anyway. She's now decided that boys don't like her because she's fat."

"She's not fat."

"I know that, and you know that, but you can't convince her of that." Daddy nodded toward the recliner next to his desk. "Let's have at those brownies."

Sophie climbed into the big chair and tucked her feet up under her. She put the milk on Daddy's desk so they could both dunk.

"How's that science project coming along?" Daddy said. "You need any more info?"

Daddy had been as good as Boppa about helping the astronauts, only instead of showing them how to make things, he taught Maggie how to set up a system for keeping track of their data—that's what he called their results—on the computer. He even gave Kitty an official NASA clipboard so she'd feel more scientific when she was following Fiona around the space station, writing down what Fiona told her to.

"I do have a question for you," Sophie said.

Daddy churned a brownie around in the milk and said, "Shoot."

"Do you ever have people on your crew disagreeing with each other?"

"Are you kidding? That's how we get to the truth of things, by debating. That's the way scientists work."

Sophie nodded in her most scientific way. "Are they ever mean to each other?"

"Some people might say that. Tempers can get pretty hot."

"What do you do then?"

Daddy chewed thoughtfully on another mouthful. So far he'd eaten three brownies to Sophie's one. They were going to need a milk refill soon.

"I tell people to go cool off," he said finally. "Then I get them back together and we look at the ideas again." Daddy grinned. "Sometimes I take a batch of your mother's cookies in with me. That almost never fails."

"Do you ever take a vote?" Sophie said.

"We vote on things like where to have lunch. Most of our decisions are made scientifically though. It's whatever is best for the project we're working on. You want some more milk?"

Sophie nodded, and Daddy headed for the kitchen. He was whistling.

That was a scathingly brilliant conversation, Sophie thought.

"I put a little chocolate syrup in it," Daddy said as he set the glass down between them again.

Sophie was glad he hadn't brought two different glasses. Sharing was — well, it wasn't scientific, but it felt good.

"So what else you got on your mind?" he said.

"Well." Sophie formed her words carefully as she watched Daddy consume another brownie. He'd also brought another stack of those from the kitchen.

"Deep subject," Daddy said.

"I just would like to know—if—everything is okay with you and Mama."

Daddy stopped with a brownie soaking in the milk. He held it in there so long Sophie was surprised it didn't fall apart.

"You don't need to worry about that, Soph," he said.

"Then everything IS okay."

"It isn't perfect. But it's going to be okay, and you don't need to worry about it."

But from the look on Daddy's face, Sophie was more convinced than ever that she did need to worry about it. His cheeks looked like they were pinching toward his ears as he set the brownie on the plate, where it wilted in a puddle of milk.

"Soph," he said, "Mama is upset. But if you keep doing what you're doing, staying in the GATE program and making those good grades and not getting in trouble, she'll feel better. Deal?"

"Deal," Sophie said. But she didn't feel like eating any more brownies. "I think I should go to bed now," she told Daddy.

"Mama will come kiss you good-night when she comes in."

Sophie hurried to her room and curled into her pillows and squeezed her eyes shut and wished she'd never asked Daddy that question. Because whatever wasn't "perfect" between Mama and him was because of her.

Captain Stella Stratos buried her face in her hands, but only for a moment. This was tragic, yes, but she had a space station to run, and a world to save. She had to sacrifice worrying about her personal problems for the good of the planet.

When that didn't do much to uncurl Sophie from her pillows, she closed her eyes again and imagined Jesus. She saw his kind eyes that understood stuff she didn't even get. His soft smile that was like Boppa's only even more pure. And his broad chest, like Daddy's, where the answers were hidden, was just a prayer away.

"Jesus, please," Sophie whispered. "I need to know how to keep Mama and Daddy from getting a divorce because I'm their problem child. And I have to keep the Corn Flakes from splitting up because of Maggie and Fiona—and ruining our whole science project and getting me kicked out of GATE. If I wait really patiently and listen for you to answer, will you tell me what to do to change everybody's mind? I figure you'll help me, because you always do."

Then she started to cry, straight into the pillows. When she heard Mama coming up the stairs, she pretended to be asleep. Seeing Sophie bawling would only upset her some more. She didn't want to imagine what would happen then.

Six

Astronaut Stella Stratos orbited through Sophie's thoughts almost all the next day at school. Fiona had to give her the cough signal twice in Ms. Quelling's social studies class — not a good place to be caught staring into the atmosphere and grabbing onto her chair so microgravity wouldn't send her floating up to the ceiling.

But at least by the time the astronauts gathered in the space station that afternoon, Stella — and Sophie — had a plan.

She announced that they were having a crew meeting.

"Why?" Maggie said.

"Because she's the captain, Nimbus," Fiona said. "She can call a crew meeting any time she wants to."

"You ready for a snack, space travelers?" said a voice from below.

Sophie leaned over the railing to see Kateesha on the ground, hooking a plastic bag over the crook in the robot-arm cane.

"Beam it up," Sophie called down.

"Roger, *Freedom 4*," Kateesha said.

Kitty giggled. "That's so cool."

"Thank you, Huntsville," Sophie said.

"Why did you call her 'Huntsville'?" Maggie said. "Her name's Kateesha."

"Our home base is in Huntsville," Sophie told her. "That's who we communicate with while we're in outer space."

They helped themselves to cookies shaped like moons and stars and rockets. Kitty giggled every time she popped one into her mouth.

"Do they eat these in space?" Maggie said.

"They do now," Fiona said.

"If I could have your attention," Captain Stella said. "Now that our space station is almost completed, we must come to a decision about comparing gravity to microgravity. I would like for each one of you to present your reasons why you want it done one way or the other and then we will vote on which idea sounds the best.

"We'll start with you, Nimbus. Please tell us your idea—"

The words instantly began to thud from Astronaut Nimbus's mouth. "I think we need something besides just building the space station to compare. The only difference is that things don't stay put in microgravity and they do here." She furrowed her forehead. "That means there's nothing for me to write down. I say we add some plants and see how they grow here and how they grow in space. I'll do that. I know about gardening. My mom and I—"

"It sounds like it's all about you," Astronaut Jupiter said.

"I can't help it if I came up with the best idea."

"What about yours, Luna?" Sophie said.

There was silence.

"Kitty," Sophie whispered.

"Oh—yeah—I'm Luna, huh?" Kitty giggled. "I'm Fiona's assistant, so I'm going to vote for whatever she says."

"Not fair," Maggie said.

"It is too fair," Fiona said. "She's taking her job very seriously."

"So what is your idea?" Captain Stella said to Jupiter.

Fiona pushed the hair out of her face. "If we try to grow plants out here, they'll freeze at night. I say we just stick with the space station."

"But then I don't get to be the record keeper," Maggie said. "It's not fair."

"It isn't about what's fair," Sophie said. "It's about what's best for the project."

"Then let's vote," Fiona said.

"All for Maggie's idea, raise your hand," Sophie said.

Maggie's arm went straight up in the air.

"All for Fiona's idea?"

Kitty and Fiona raised their hands, and Kitty grabbed Fiona's, the way Sophie had seen people running for president do with their wives on TV.

"Not fair," Maggie said.

"How is that not fair?" Fiona said. "It's two against one."

"Sophie didn't vote."

They all looked at Captain Stella, who swallowed a large lump of a moon cookie.

"Whose side are you on?" Maggie said.

"Like I said, I want what's best for the project," Sophie said. She swallowed again. *How does Daddy do this every single day?* she thought.

"So vote," Maggie said.

"Okay. I think Astronaut Jupiter's idea is the best. Only we could make it so that—"

"Not fair."

Fiona turned to Maggie, nostrils in a record-breaking flare.

"You know what, NIMbus?" she said. "You're just mad because you didn't get your own way. That isn't very scientific."

"This whole project is just gonna be dumb now," Maggie said.

And with that final thudding sentence, she snatched up her backpack and disappeared down the ladder. The other three Corn Flakes waited until they heard her land heavily in "Huntsville" before they said a word.

Fiona let out a huge relief-sigh. "Good riddance is what I say."

"Me too," Kitty said. "She's way too bossy."

But Sophie shook her head. "Who's going to keep the records?"

"We won't have any records, remember?" Fiona said.

"I was going to tell you guys how we could do it so she'd have stuff to write down," Sophie said, "but she didn't even wait for me to finish."

"Luna can do it," Fiona said.

Kitty's face froze up. "Me? I can't spell that good and my handwriting stinks."

"It doesn't matter ..." Sophie started to tell her.

And then she stopped. Fiona's eyes went into slits, and Sophie felt her stomach churn. She had never seen her best friend look so much like a Corn Pop. This Fiona was wearing a face that said, *Don't mess with me. I'll get my way.*

"The only problem," Fiona said, in a voice that matched her eyes, "is that Maggie took all of our plans with her. I hope she doesn't try to sell them to the enemy."

"We have enemies?" Kitty said.

As Astronaut Jupiter went on to explain that there were always intergalactic villains flying around at light speed, Captain Stella Stratos closed her eyes.

We have had a mutiny, just as I feared, she thought. *What's to be done? When the head of NASA, Commander Utley, finds out that Astronaut Nimbus has left the program, we will be called in for questioning. I do not want to tell her that there has been too much fighting among the Expedition Crew. That violates the code of the Corn Flake Society: we will not leave anyone out.* Captain Stratos looked out into deep space. *I feel responsible for Astronaut Nimbus. What is she to do for a project? And can we save the planet without her?*

Sophie's stomach churned even more. And what about Fiona? Why was she suddenly like the people Sophie always daydreamed her way away from?

Captain Stella put her hands up to her space helmet and checked its arrangement on her head. She was certainly glad that she had an appointment with the NASA psychologist the next day. Scientist Peter Topping would know exactly what to do.

Mama went up to the Loom Room again after supper that night, and even though Daddy made popcorn and invited everybody to watch *Finding Nemo* with him after they did their homework, Sophie felt like there was a big old hole in the family room where Mama should have been. Lacie wanted to watch *Clueless* for about the seventy-fifth time, and when Daddy said "unh-uh" (and Zeke howled the longest "NO-O-O" in history), Lacie stomped upstairs and slammed her bedroom door.

Daddy looked at Sophie over the head of Zeke, who was still hollering, and said, "You're the only sane person left in this family."

Even that didn't wipe out Sophie's worries.

Mama made them worse the next morning by being way quiet while everybody was getting ready for school. She didn't even say much when Zeke put his socks on his ears instead of his feet and stuck a raisin into each nostril.

I wonder if she's daydreaming, Sophie thought. *I hope she's not imagining leaving us.*

The pang in her chest went straight through to her backbone. She couldn't blow this science project, or Mama would get upset. She couldn't do anything that would let Mama go. That just couldn't happen. Sophie climbed off her stool at the snack bar and knelt down beside Zeke.

"I'll put his shoes and socks on him, Mama," she said.

Mama mumbled a "thank you" and went back to the lunch boxes, where she was making peanut butter and jelly sandwiches again.

Between that and the memory of Fiona with slanted eyes and sneery voice, it was impossible not to let Captain Stella Stratos take over during the school day. Sophie imagined Jesus too, and she begged him again to help her fix things. But he just kept smiling his kind smile and didn't give her any answers.

In second period Ms. Quelling made them read, and most of the class had their faces in their social studies books, except for the Fruit Loops. Tod was acting like he was reading, but Sophie could see him giving directions to the other two Loops with his sharp little eyes. Colton kept leaning under his desk like he was trying to find something, and when he seemed to get his hands on it he slipped it to Eddie. Sophie was expecting them to take the whole class hostage any minute.

That's exactly the sort of thing we need to save the planet from, Captain Stella Stratos thought. *The secret plans of Moron-oids who want to take over the universe and make people bow down to them and feed them Cheetos.*

Captain Stella adjusted her glasses. She was going to have to be prepared to evacuate the room when the Moron-oids opened fire with their secret space weapons. If only she knew what they were. It was hard to defend a planet against the unknown. So far, all she had been able to figure out from their presence was that they had brains they seldom used except to humiliate the citizens of earth. And that they had a peculiar smell. And that they could not be trusted.

She needed to get closer now, where she could possibly gather data.

Stella crept in clandestine fashion around the back of the Huntsville control room, keeping out of sight of the Moron-oids. As she drew closer to their corner, she paused, making certain that she wasn't seen. She glanced at her official Freedom 4 watch. It was ten hundred hours. She would need to make a note of that in her report.

But in the instant she took her eyes from the Moron-oids, the three space villains had gotten off a shot. Several small green projectiles were thrust from a tube planted firmly in Moron-oid Eddie's nose.

Those could be weapons of mass destruction! Captain Stella thought. With the lightning speed of a finely tuned scientific mind, she made a decision. Diving from her place against the wall, she hurled herself forward and grasped for the green bullet that was even then piercing through the air. It didn't matter that she herself could be mortally wounded. She couldn't let anyone else be hurt.

The bullet hit the palm of her hand, and she curled her fingers around it just as gravity pushed her to the floor. Even before she hit the ground she could feel the tiny green object giving way to a soft mush in her hand. It could be some form of biological warfare—

Or it could be a pea. Sophie sat on the floor, right at the feet of Julia Cummings, and stared at her open palm. A green mass was squished right in the middle.

"Gross me out!" Julia said.

"What is going on?" Ms. Quelling called out from her desk.

Sophie could hardly hear her over the racket that was coming from the Fruit Loops' corner. Their monkey-laughter shrieked right up to the ozone layer. Eddie fell out of his desk.

Seven

Ms. Quelling stood over Sophie, looking down between two thick curtains of bronze-colored hair.

"Sophie," she said. *"What on earth?"* Then she looked at Julia, eyebrows up.

"I don't know," Julia said. "She just threw herself down here like some kind of freak." She put up both hands, spreading out her fingers with Valentine-red fingernails. "I didn't do anything to her, I swear."

"All right, get up off the ground, for starters," Ms. Quelling said to Sophie.

She didn't appear to notice that Eddie was still rolling on the floor, his face as red as Julia's manicure. By the time Sophie got to her feet, she was aware that the whole class had their faces in their books and their eyes over the tops of the pages on her. The entire room seemed to be holding its breath.

"What in the world were you doing?" Ms. Quelling said. Her forehead was twisted into a question mark.

"I was catching this," Sophie said, opening her hand. "Eddie was shooting them out of his nose."

Julia coiled up and slapped the red nails over her mouth.

"It's a good thing I did too," Sophie said to her, "because it was headed straight for the side of your face."

Ms. Quelling turned to the Fruit Loops. "Is this true, boys? Where is Eddie?"

Tod and Colton both pointed calmly to the floor.

"Eddie! Get up!" Ms. Quelling said.

"I can't!" Eddie said. "I think I laughed myself to death."

I hope so, Sophie thought.

"Is this your pea, Eddie?" Ms. Quelling said.

That did it. The class let out its held-back breath in one enormous burst of hysteria. Ms. Quelling closed her eyes, and Sophie could see her trying not to join in.

"All right, go wash your hand, Sophie," Ms. Quelling said. "Eddie, come up to my desk, and bring your peas with you."

"He doesn't have them," Sophie said. "Colton does."

Ms. Quelling gave Sophie a pointy look, as if Sophie hadn't just made her life easier by giving her all the information she needed. "I will talk to *you* later," she said.

Later didn't happen right away, which meant Sophie couldn't think about anything else through the rest of her morning classes except that Ms. Quelling was after her again. By lunchtime, Sophie could barely choke down her peanut butter and jelly sandwich.

"I don't see why you would get in trouble," Kitty said. "You were just trying to save Julia."

"The question is, why?" Fiona said.

Maggie would probably have jumped right in and reminded Fiona that the Corn Flakes tried to protect everybody from harm. But Maggie hadn't hung out with them all day. Right now she was sitting alone all the way at the other end of the table, past the Wheaties, putting one tortilla chip after another into her mouth like letters into a mail slot.

"Uh-oh," Kitty said. "Here comes Ms. Quelling. I think you're busted, Sophie."

Ms. Quelling stopped at the end of the table, forehead twisted into that question mark thing like it had been there since second period. Fiona squeezed Sophie's hand.

"You were right, Sophie," Ms. Quelling said. "Eddie and Colton were doing their boy thing. I've dealt with them."

"And Tod?" Sophie said.

"What does Tod have to do with it?"

"He put them up to it. I saw him."

"Which brings me to why you were lurking on that side of the room in the first place, Sophie," Ms. Quelling said. "You were supposed to be reading."

Sophie didn't answer. Ms. Quelling would never understand about a scientific thing.

"Never mind," Ms. Quelling said. "I know what you were up to. Now that Julia and B.J. and Anne-Stuart have changed and you can't blame everything on them anymore, you're looking for ways to get the boys in trouble."

"I wasn't doing that!" Sophie said.

"Trust me, Ms. Quelling," Fiona said, her gray eyes wide and serious. "I know Sophie. She would never do that."

"Thank you, Fiona," Ms. Quelling said coldly. "When Sophie needs a character witness, I'm sure she'll call you." She lowered her sights on Sophie again like she was aiming a rifle. "I'm going to let it go this time, but from now on, you'd better leave those boys alone. Don't think you can do this kind of thing and stay in the GATE program."

They don't leave us alone! Sophie wanted to say.

As Ms. Quelling strode out of the cafeteria—amid calls from the Corn Pops of "Hi, Ms. Quelling! Love you!"—Kitty turned frightened eyes on Sophie.

"Why does she hate you so much?"

"Because Sophie has proved her wrong twice before about her little teacher's pets," Fiona said. "She can't tolerate being wrong."

"I know what 'tolerate' means," Kitty said. "You should leave them alone, Sophie."

"I'm not doing anything to them! They're the ones doing it all!"

"Besides," Fiona said, "we vowed we could handle them, and we will."

"How can we do that when we can't even talk to them?" Kitty said.

Nobody had an answer for that.

"I can't figure out why they're all of a sudden picking on you," Fiona said to Sophie. "Up 'til, like, two weeks ago, they acted like we didn't even exist."

"I wish they still did," Kitty said.

"Let's just pretend THEY don't exist," Sophie said. "That's how we'll handle them. It isn't bad to leave them out and not be friendly to them and stuff. They're boys."

Besides, there was the space station to think about. They had to give a progress report in science that afternoon, and Maggie had their plan.

"I'm just gonna go ask her for it," Fiona said when they got to P.E.

Sophie had a sudden vision of another almost-fistfight right there on the playground.

"No—I'll think of something—scientific," she said. "I'm the captain."

A basketball bounced by, and as Fiona turned to run after it, she murmured to Sophie, "Pretty soon, it's just going to be the original Corn Flakes again." The smile she gave Sophie wasn't Fiona-luscious.

Sophie's thoughts went straight for Captain Stella, but she was barely able to get her into focus when the basketball suddenly knocked her in the head and set her on her tail on the concrete. It was Maggie who pulled her up and asked her if she was okay.

"I'm fine," Sophie said.

"Let me look at your eyes," Maggie said.

Sophie stared as Maggie squinted critically into her face.

"I don't think you have a concussion," she said.

"How do you know, Nimbus?" Fiona said.

"I have a first-aid card. My mom and I went to a class together."

"Wow," Kitty said. "That's cool."

First aid. Suddenly, Sophie had an idea.

"I know you're upset about my decision yesterday, Nimbus," she said. "But I want you to consider the whole crew. With your medical knowledge, you could actually save our lives if we got into trouble."

Maggie hesitated for a minute, pressing her lips together. "I would need to put my first-aid kit in the space station," she said.

"Of course," Captain Stella said. "Anything you need. Right, Expedition Crew?"

Kitty looked at Fiona. Even though Fiona pulled her lips into a knot, she finally nodded.

Sophie was feeling better about everything when she got into the Suburban that afternoon so Mama could take her to see Dr. Peter. At LAST. And when Mama smiled at her, she felt even better.

"Hey, Dream Girl," Mama said. "I want to thank you for helping with Zeke this morning. I know I haven't been myself lately, and you gave me a little lift."

Does that mean you aren't leaving us? Sophie wanted to say. Instead, she said, "I'll help any time you want, Mama. I could give him his bath and read him books and clean up his room—"

Mama gave her a blank stare before she smiled again. "Don't overdo it, Sophie," she said. "You'll have me thinking you're trying to butter me up for something!" She squeezed Sophie's knee. "Now—how was your day? Anything exciting happen?"

The incident with Eddie and the peas ran through Sophie's head, chased by the scene with Ms. Quelling in the cafeteria. She would tell Mama about that later, when she knew she was completely better. When she started making good lunches again and coming to tuck Sophie in at night.

But Sophie did bring it up with Dr. Peter the minute she was settled in on his window seat and had one of his face pillows on her lap. She chose the one with the fuzzy blue hair so she could comb her fingers through it and not chew her own hair while she talked.

"Whoa, Sophie-Lophie-Loodle," Dr. Peter said. "Start from the beginning. Tell me all about this Captain Stella Stratos." His twinkly blue eyes shone through the lenses of his wire-rimmed glasses. It was one of about a thousand things she liked about him. He wore glasses too, and he was still about the most awesome grown-up she knew.

Sophie launched into a detailed account of Captain Stella and the space station and her recent issues with her crew. The whole time, Dr. Peter watched her and nodded his head of cut-short, reddish brown hair. When she was finished, Dr. Peter picked up the face pillow with the orange puffs of hair that came out of its nostrils.

"Sounds like our Loodle is going off to Sophie World in school again," he said to it. "What do you think?"

The pillow nodded. Dr. Peter looked at Sophie. "Why is that?"

"Because we have to get our project done. It's very complex. It requires a lot of concentration."

"You haven't by any chance forgotten your agreement with your dad, have you?"

"You mean only going into Sophie World when I'm filming?" Sophie sighed. "I am filming. AND I'm imagining Jesus. But it's not helping."

"Okay," Dr. Peter said. "You want to do a treasure hunt and find out why?"

That was another reason she liked Dr. Peter. He never even looked like he thought she was loony tunes.

"Okay," she said. "Only, could we make it like exploring outer space instead? I'm really into that right now."

"Of course. Silly me," he said. "Now—I want you to close your eyes and imagine you're going through space in your capsule."

That was easy. Stars and planets began to zip by in her mind.

"Now, as you know, Captain," he went on, "sometimes meteors go through space and leave a trail of debris on things they hit."

"Is any of it going to hit my capsule?" Sophie said.

"It may. If that happens, you need to stop and see what it was and how much damage it has done. Then you can decide if you can fix it."

"Yes, sir," Sophie said.

"All right, proceed through space and let me know when something collides with your craft."

Sophie opened one eye. "What if I ask Jesus not to let anything hit me?"

"You can ask that. But it might be better to ask him to keep you from being damaged when something hits you. Outer space is filled with flying objects for reasons we don't even understand—even though we're scientists. Being strong enough to handle them all is what we need to ask for."

Sophie closed her eyes again and almost immediately she imagined something hitting square in the middle of the space capsule's window.

"Reduce speed, Captain, and let's examine it."

"Do I open my eyes?" Sophie said.

"Whatever helps you see best."

Sophie kept her eyes squeezed shut and let herself imagine the big rock that had split apart against the space-worthy glass.

"What do you think it is?" Dr. Peter said.

"I can't tell."

She could picture Dr. Peter's nose wrinkling to push up his glasses. "It looks to me like a piece of a family," he said.

"A family? You mean, like, people?"

"It's more like an idea of a family."

"Oh," Sophie said. "And it came apart."

Suddenly, she felt squirmy, and her chest hurt.

"Permission to move on, Huntsville," Sophie said. "I have decided my capsule wasn't damaged."

"Loodle," Dr. Peter said. He was using his soft come-back-to-earth voice.

Sophie hugged the pillow to her chest and opened her eyes.

"I don't want to talk about families falling apart, Dr. Peter," she said.

"Is that because you're afraid your family is falling apart?"

Sophie nodded.

"You want to tell me about it?"

No, she didn't. But the words came out anyway, in one big blurt.

"Zeke is acting out all over the place like he's Terrible Two again," she said. "Lacie is being all weird about boys. Daddy says I'm the only sane one left in the family."

"What about your father? Is he being 'all weird'?"

Sophie shook her head. "We're getting along better than ever in my whole entire life." She hugged the pillow until its nose dug into her stomach. She knew what Dr. Peter's next question was going to be.

"And how about your mama?" he said.

"I think she's gonna leave us! She hardly laughs or talks, and she acts like she's always mad at Daddy. And it's all my fault!"

"Your fault?" Dr. Peter said. "You want to tell me why you think that?"

"Daddy told me if I kept making good grades and staying out of trouble, she would feel better. That's why I didn't tell her about what happened today. She might just pack her suitcase and go. I would hate it without her. She's my mama!"

Sophie didn't realize until then that she was crying. Dr. Peter handed her a Kleenex out of a box with moons and stars on it.

Sophie plastered one over her eyes and cried into it some more. Dr. Peter just waited. When she looked up at him, he was studying her carefully.

"You know, Loodle," he said, "I almost never tell you that you're wrong."

"Are you going to now?" Sophie said.

"I am." He leaned forward. "You are so wrong about anything between your mother and father being your fault. Or Zeke's, or Lacie's."

"But I don't want her to leave for any reason. I'm trying to fix it. I'm helping with Zeke when he starts acting like a little brat, and I'm not fighting with Lacie. But I already miss Mama, and she isn't even gone yet."

Dr. Peter nodded. "Do you feel like she's gone because she isn't with you like she used to be with you?"

"Yes!" Sophie said.

"You know something, Loodle?" he said. "You sometimes know things about people they haven't even figured out about themselves."

Sophie felt the pain in her chest again. "Then she is going to leave. I have to stop her!"

"Now hang on," Dr. Peter said. "All I'm saying is that you seem to understand that she is taking a little mental trip right now, just like you do when you get scared about things and go into Sophie World."

"What's she scared of?" Sophie said.

"That I can't tell you. But I think you're the best person in the house to understand about wanting to escape."

Sophie straightened her shoulders. "I can help her then. I'll give her a signal when she starts drifting off, like Fiona coughs when she sees me zoning out in school."

Dr. Peter's face grew serious. "I don't want you to try to fix your mother, okay, Loodle? First of all, that isn't your job. It's God's."

"But I keep asking him to fix it and he doesn't!"

"I think he's working on it. In fact, I'm sure of it. What do you say we let him do his job and you do yours? Just like the astronauts on your crew."

"But what's my job?" Sophie said.

Dr. Peter's eyes twinkled again. "I think it's time to get to know Jesus a little bit better so you can see how God handles stuff like this."

"Back to the Bible," Sophie said.

"You're brilliant," Dr. Peter said, handing her a piece of paper with Bible verses written on it. "That must be why they made you captain of the spaceship. Now remember, read the story and imagine yourself playing one of the parts."

"I can do that."

"Yes, you can. And I'm going to give you a little hint—pay attention to what the little kid does and what Jesus does with that."

"Roger," Sophie said.

She wasn't crying when she left Dr. Peter's office. She had the Bible verses tucked in her pocket, and a new idea tucked in her head.

It's like another mission. God is Huntsville, and I'm flying the space capsule.

She was almost smiling when she met Daddy in the waiting room. One look at his face, though, and the desire to grin shattered like a piece of space debris. His mouth was in a tight line she hadn't seen there since the last time she was in big trouble.

Eight

Daddy didn't say anything until they got into the truck, and Sophie didn't ask him any questions. But as soon as he pulled out into Hampton traffic, he said, "I thought we had a deal."

Sophie readjusted her glasses to peer at him. "We do!" she said. "I'm not even making any C's right now."

"You will be soon if you pull another stunt like you did in school today."

A mental picture of Julia showing up at the LaCroix's front door telling all flashed through Sophie's mind.

"Ms. Quelling called to tell me that you almost tackled somebody to catch a pea some kid shot out of a straw, just to get the kid in trouble."

"That isn't what happened!" Sophie said.

"I know that isn't what happened. What happened was you got so wrapped up in one of your daydreams you started acting it out, and suddenly there you were, sprawled out on the floor with a smashed vegetable in your hand." Daddy pulled up to a red light and lowered his eyebrows at her. "That's what happened, right?"

"Yes!" Sophie said. "But it won't happen again. I promise."

"Do you need a little reminder? Do I need to take the camera away for a while?"

Sophie tried to remain calm, although she had to clutch the door handle to do it.

"No," she said. "Dr. Peter helped me with that today."

Daddy was quiet for a few blocks. Sophie chewed her hair and swung her legs against the seat. Her feet didn't touch the floor in Daddy's truck as it was, and she was feeling smaller by the minute.

"It isn't just about your grades, Soph," Daddy said. "I told you I didn't want you upsetting your mother."

"Does she know about this?" Sophie said.

"No. Ms. Quelling called me at work."

"She interrupted you trying to save the planet to tell you that?"

Sophie thought she saw the corners of Daddy's mouth twitch.

"Yeah," he said. "And I think she enjoyed it." He shot Sophie a Daddy-look. "But that doesn't mean you didn't mess up."

"Am I going to get a punishment?" she said.

"Definitely."

Sophie felt her heart take a dive. It probably wasn't going to be as bad as banishment from the planet, but still.

"Tonight, after you finish your homework," Daddy said, "you have to bring a glass of milk and exactly twelve cookies to my study and stay there until they're all gone."

"I can endure that."

"Is that a Fiona word?" Daddy said.

"Yes, sir," Sophie said.

She waited until she got up to her room after supper to really sigh, so Daddy wouldn't think that she thought she was getting off easy. The feeling didn't last long though. Fiona called, puffing like a bull on the other end of the line.

"Huntsville, we have a problem," she said.

"What is it, Jupiter?" Sophie said.

"I just went up to *Freedom 4* to get my backpack I left up there after we were working today—and the robot arm was totally torn off."

Sophie gasped. "Did the wind do it?"

"There was no wind today."

"Didn't we attach it right?"

"It didn't happen by itself," Fiona said. "Boppa went up there and looked at it. He said somebody tore it off!"

Sophie's tongue went stiff. "Who would do that? Oh—it was Rory and Isabella, huh?"

"No—they were at the library with Kateesha all afternoon. Besides, I know who did this, and so do you."

"I do?"

"It was so Maggie. She brought costumes today, by the way—"

"Are they amazing?"

"They look just like the pictures," Fiona said. "But that isn't the point."

Sophie could almost see Fiona's eyes going into Corn Pop slits.

"She was even pretty decent when she and Kitty were up in the space station with me," Fiona said, "but that was just an act. She's still mad because we didn't do it her way."

Sophie was shaking her head as if Fiona could see her through the phone. "It doesn't make sense. If she messed it up, it would ruin her grade too."

"That's just it. She thinks she's going to tell us how to fix it and she'll get her way because our way didn't work, and when we get a good grade she'll say it was all because of her. We could even get taken out of GATE for not doing more work than her." Fiona gave a hard little laugh. "But I have news for her. Boppa already fixed it. He said it was something we couldn't do and he'll explain it to Mrs. Utley. I'm sure glad Ms. Quelling isn't our science teacher." Fiona finally took a breath. "So what are you going to do now?"

"Me?"

"You're the captain. You need to have a plan or Maggie is going to keep doing things until she ruins it for all of us. I think you should call a meeting of just you, me, and Luna, and tell us what you want us to do."

Sophie mumbled something and hung up and closed her eyes. Jesus showed up right away, looking at her with kind eyes.

"Is this your job or mine?" she whispered to him.

He didn't answer of course, but it did make her think of the Bible story Dr. Peter had told her to read. That was supposed to be about the Mama Mission, but she needed some help with this mission or it was going to fall completely apart.

Sophie pulled her Bible out and propped up against her pile of plump pillows. She noted that she and Dr. Peter were both into big cushions. Another reason she liked him so much.

It wasn't hard to find John 6, verses 1 through 13. Since before Christmas, Dr. Peter had her read a Bible story almost every time she saw him and she was getting good at finding her way around.

Jesus crossed to the far shore of the Sea of Galilee, she read, *and a great crowd of people followed him because they saw the miraculous signs he had performed on the sick.*

Sophie could already imagine herself as one of them. Any minute now he would perform a miraculous sign for her and fix this whole space-station dilemma. She got a picture in her head of herself in a little purple robe and a rope belt and sandals.

When Jesus looked up and saw a great crowd coming toward him, he said to Philip, "Where shall we buy bread for these people to eat?" He asked this only to test him, for he already had in mind what he was going to do.

Sophie was glad she hadn't imagined herself as Philip. She didn't know the answer to that question.

Philip answered him, "Eight months' wages would not buy enough bread for each one to have a bite!"

Another of his disciples, Andrew, Simon Peter's brother, spoke up. "Here is a boy with five small barley loaves and two small fish, but how far will they go among so many?"

Sophie thought that must be the little kid Dr. Peter had mentioned. She decided it was okay if she made the boy a girl. Quickly she created a picture in her mind of her sandal-footed self, holding up a couple of fish and five very small loaves of bread. She wasn't sure what barley was, but she mentally sprinkled some seeds on top of the loaves and let it go at that. The important thing was the feeling she was already getting in her chest, like her heart was so afraid Jesus wouldn't like what she had to offer. But after all, she was the only one in the whole crowd who had bothered to bring a lunch.

Jesus said, "Have the people sit down." There was plenty of grass in that place, and the men sat down, about five thousand of them. Jesus then took the loaves, gave thanks, and distributed to those who were seated as much as they wanted. He did the same with the fish.

Sophie breathed a huge sigh. He liked the lunch, or he wouldn't be giving thanks for it. She took a few seconds to imagine Jesus holding the little rolls up toward heaven and saying, "God is great, God is good. Now we thank you for this food." The smell of them wafted down to her nose. She was starting to get hungry.

It was one of those all-you-can-eat things, Sophie thought. All Daddy could eat was enough for about three people. If there were five thousand like him, that was a lot of food. Sophie closed her eyes and saw it all, steaming loaves being passed to the ones in the back who thought they wouldn't get even a crumb. Herself running up and down the rows, grass tickling her stuck-out toes as she handed out basket after basket of fish until everyone was groaning because they'd completely pigged out.

Opening her eyes, she continued. *When they had all had enough to eat, he said to his disciples, "Gather the pieces that are left over. Let nothing be wasted." So they gathered them*—with Sophie helping—*and filled twelve baskets with the pieces of the five barley loaves left over by those who had eaten.*

Sophie closed the Bible on her lap, but she kept her eyes open. The story was as clear as if it had happened right down at Buckroe Beach, but she knew her forehead was wrinkled into about five thousand folds.

What's that got to do with Mama—or the Freedom 4—*or any other problem I have?* she thought. *I don't get it.*

She wished Dr. Peter were there so he could explain it to her. With Fiona and Kitty expecting a plan tomorrow morning, she didn't have time to wait two weeks for her next appointment. She ran her finger down the wrinkles in her forehead as she tried to imagine his voice, coaching her. All that came were the words he'd already said to her that afternoon.

Pay attention to what the little kid does and what Jesus does with that.

Sophie went back to her imagination. The little kid was her. What had she done?

"I gave up my lunch," she said out loud. "It wasn't that much, but it was all Mama had packed for me. That must have been the Bible-days version of peanut butter and jelly sandwiches."

She dived back in. What had Jesus done with it?

Du-uh, she thought. *He fed, like, a bazillion people. He put his hands up with the bread and the fish in them and he gave thanks. And whammo—it was enough for a feast.*

Sophie gnawed at her hair. Was she supposed to take lunch for the Corn Flakes tomorrow? No, that couldn't be it. What else had Dr. Peter said about God?

What do you say we let him do his job and you do yours?

"Okay, so I bring one sandwich and he makes it enough for the whole cafeteria. No—la-ame."

Sophie devoured several split ends before she gave up and went downstairs to take the twelve cookies and one glass of milk to Daddy. She was tempted to ask him what he would do, but she decided that wasn't the best move. She wasn't supposed to try to fix Mama, but she didn't want to make her worse. If Mama found out there was trouble among the Corn Flakes and they might fail their science project if they didn't make it better, she would definitely be upset.

On the way down the steps, Sophie switched back to Jesus. *I guess I'm back to "you show me my job and I'll do it, and I'll let you do yours."*

And could you please hurry up?

The next morning Sophie got a ride with Daddy instead of taking the bus so she could get to school way early. The sun wasn't shining except for a blur in the gray clouds, struggling to seep through, and there was frost on everything. Sophie found Kitty and Fiona backstage in the cafeteria, where they always met in bad weather, sitting in the middle of some old set pieces that they had pulled together to make a closed-off place.

Kitty jumped like somebody had popped a balloon when Sophie said, "Hi!" and she banged her head on a wooden tree. Fiona put her finger up to her lips.

"We're trying to keep a low profile," she whispered.

"We're also being very quiet," Kitty said.

Sophie nodded solemnly and slipped in between them. She wasn't even worried about floor dust getting on her khakis. This was serious stuff, and so far Jesus hadn't given her so much as a hint of a plan.

"So what are we going to do?" Fiona said, voice low.

"We don't even know if it was really Maggie who broke the robot arm," Sophie said.

"I know," Fiona said.

"Can we prove it?"

Fiona's dark eyebrows squeezed together over her nose. "You mean, like, fingerprints or something?"

"We have to be scientific about it," Sophie said. "Besides, if we accuse her and it turns out she didn't do it, we could get into big trouble."

Fiona folded her arms stubbornly across her chest. "I still say it's Maggie. It has her name all over it. And how are we going to protect our project with her still involved in it?"

Sophie nibbled at the ends of her braids.

"The only way is to get rid of her," Fiona said.

"Like throw her over the side of the tree house?" Kitty said. Her eyes were bulging like a terrified bullfrog's.

"Hello! No!" Fiona put her hand over her mouth and looked toward the opening in the curtain.

"What?" Sophie said.

"I just don't want Maggie to hear us. You know she'll be looking for us any minute." She leaned in, and so did Kitty and Sophie. "I mean, we have to prove she did it and then Mrs. Utley will take her off the project."

Sophie knew what to say now. "It's not our job to prove Maggie did it. Our job is to show how microgravity is different."

"And how are we going to make sure it doesn't get sabotaged?" Fiona said.

"Does that mean 'torn up'?" Kitty said.

Fiona had barely nodded when Sophie heard a voice thudding from the direction of the cafeteria door.

"Sophie? Fiona? You guys in here?"

"So what's the plan?" Fiona whispered.

"I'll get back to you," Sophie squeaked back.

"But we can't talk about it with her around," Fiona said.

"We could pass notes," Kitty said. "We used to do it all the time when I was a Corn Pop."

"I would get caught," Sophie said. "I can't do anything without getting caught. It's a curse."

"You guys?" Maggie's voice was getting louder and closer. According to Sophie's calculations, she would be on the stage in five seconds.

"I'll take that job," Fiona whispered. "If you get any ideas, just write them down and stick them in my pocket between classes. Then I'll put together a list."

Four, three, two, one —

"In here, Nimbus!" Sophie called out.

Maggie stuck her head through the opening in the curtain. Sophie hoped they didn't all look as guilty as she felt.

Nine

✳ ⌂ ✺

By the time second-period social studies was over Fiona had so many notes stuffed into her side jeans pockets she looked to Sophie like she had an extra set of hips. When Maggie came up behind them in the hall, Fiona turned to her, walking backward.

"Hi, Maggie," Fiona said.

"What's going on?" Maggie said. "You guys are acting all weird."

Kitty shot Sophie a whimpering look. Fiona's glance clearly said, *Uh-oh*.

"See?" Maggie said to Sophie. "It's like you have some kinda secret or something."

Suddenly Sophie felt like she was one of the Corn Pops, about to squeal out, *Oh, no, Maggie, we would never keep a secret from you.*

It made her want to hiss at herself. This definitely wasn't the job she was supposed to be doing. She linked her arm through Maggie's and held on as they walked, even though Maggie stiffened up as if Sophie were trying to freeze-dry her.

"We didn't want to upset you," Sophie said. "But you should know."

Fiona suddenly sounded like she was choking to death. Kitty was now whimpering out loud.

"Know what?" Maggie said.

They stopped outside the door to the computer room.

"Somebody tore the robot arm off the *Freedom 4* yesterday," Sophie said.

"Who?" Maggie said.

Fiona gave Sophie a what-are-you-doing stare.

"We don't know who did it," Sophie said. "But we have to protect the project."

"You mean, like, set up a stakeout?"

The whining, whimpering, and choking all stopped. The three other Corn Flakes stared at Maggie.

"Tell me some more," Sophie said.

"Write it in a note," Fiona said. "The bell's gonna ring."

Not that Mrs. Yacanovich ever noticed people coming in late. It took her half the period just to call the roll and get people to stop hollering things across the room to one another long enough to give the assignment. That gave all the Corn Flakes a chance to whip off notes. The only thing Sophie was worried about then was getting them mixed up with the ones the Corn Pops were delivering to each other. They actually had it down to a science, Sophie noticed. Julia could write a half-page letter and get replies back from Willoughby, B.J., and Anne-Stuart in the time it took Sophie to get one folded. They'd obviously had a lot more practice.

Maggie wrote a note to Sophie, folded it up into a perfect triangle, and dropped it next to her computer. Before Sophie could even reach for it, Colton came out of nowhere and snatched it up. He shot it like a basketball toward the corner trash can.

Fortunately, Colton was no basketball player. The note missed by about half a classroom and landed right on top of Anne-Stuart's computer monitor. Good fortune was with them again, because Anne-Stuart was, of course, blowing her nose at the time, and didn't get to it before Kitty leaped from her chair and grabbed it. She looked at Anne-Stuart and said, "Sorry—wrong address!" Then she giggled and flipped around in time to avoid Mrs. Y. who was chasing Eddie Wornom down the aisle. He had her grade book.

But Sophie saw that more trouble was coming Kitty's way in the form of Tod.

"Kitty!" she hissed. Although how Kitty was supposed to hear her over the classroom racket was beyond her.

When Tod kept dodging stuck-out feet and elbows with eyes riveted on that note in Kitty's hand, Sophie scrambled up to her knees in the chair and waved her arms.

"Give it up, LaCroix," said a male voice at her elbow. "You'll never get off the ground."

Sophie whipped her head around to look at Colton. In that nanosecond there was a Kitty-squeal. Sophie forgot Colton, who was now imitating her like an out-of-control flamingo. Tod had the note and was continuing down the aisle, head back, balancing it on his Whoville nose. Which was why he didn't notice Mrs. Y. holding her hands over her head, about to explode. When she yelled, "Class! QUIET!" he jerked his head up and the note fell into Mrs. Y.'s oncoming path. Sophie gasped, and she could hear Fiona doing the same. Kitty was whining like a cocker spaniel.

Mrs. Y. stopped right in front of Tod—and stepped on the little triangle.

"Now!" she said. "Everyone take your seat— immediately!"

There was a mass-scurry as if an anthill had just been destroyed. The only person who had been sitting the whole time was Maggie. But she'd seen it all, Sophie knew, because she, like the rest of the Corn Flakes, was staring at Mrs. Y.'s left loafer with horror in her eyes.

"I'm no longer going to yell to be heard in this classroom!" Mrs. Y.—well—yelled. "Everyone start Microsoft Word and do not speak a single syllable while you're doing it."

Fiona turned to Sophie with her lips already in mid-whisper.

"Not that kind of micro-soft word, Fiona," Mrs. Y. said.

Colton let out a laugh like the kind on TV commercials. "You're really funny, Mrs. Y."

"Yeah, I'm a real crack-up. Now get to work."

The whole class lowered their faces behind their monitors except for the Corn Flakes, who peeked out from the sides to watch Mrs. Y.'s left loafer. The teacher turned to march down the aisle, and the note went with her. It was stuck to the bottom of her shoe.

"We're doomed," Fiona mouthed to Sophie.

Sophie couldn't even mouth back, "Oh, we so are."

After that, it was hard to type and keep track of Mrs. Y.'s constantly moving heel at the same time. The Corn Flakes automatically took turns, and they weren't the only ones.

When Mrs. Y. passed Colton, he pretended to be picking up his pencil—who used a pencil in computer class?—and tried to grab the note. To Sophie's immense relief, he missed. Eddie looked like he was going to shoot a rubber band at it, until Tod hit him over the head with his mouse. Sophie couldn't figure out how Mrs. Y. didn't see that. No wonder the class was a zoo most of the time.

Sophie and the other Corn Flakes were all still watching the progress of the note and the loafer when Maggie tapped Mrs. Y. on the arm.

"You have something stuck on the bottom of your shoe," she said.

Sophie's fingers froze on the keyboard.

"Oh," Mrs. Y. said. She reached down and pulled the note off. "Thanks."

Fiona looked Sophie full in the face and mouthed, "It's OVER."

Sophie closed her eyes, but before she could even beam up Captain Stella Stratos she heard Fiona let out the sigh of the century. When Sophie looked around, Mrs. Y. was tossing their little triangle into the trash can.

Nearby, there was a thud. Eddie Wornom had fallen off his chair.

WHAT HAPPENED? Sophie typed on her screen.

HE WAS LEANING OUT TO WATCH HER AND HE FELL, Fiona wrote back. KLUTZ.

What is so interesting about one of our notes? Sophie thought. *Do I have a sign on my back that says, "Drive Sophie crazy"?*

Sophie looked around to see how the Fruit Loops were reacting. Tod was typing away with a too-innocent look on his face. Colton was looking at somebody and shrugging his shoulders. He was all but saying, *What do you want from me?*

The somebody was Julia.

When the bell finally rang for lunch, Sophie stepped out into the hall to meet the rest of the Corn Flakes.

"That was so close!" Kitty said. Her face was pale to the tip of her nose as she looked at Maggie. "I thought we'd had it when you told her!"

Fiona too was looking at Maggie. Although Sophie knew it pained her to do it, Fiona said, "That was pretty smart, Nimbus. Good call."

"I try," Maggie said. As always, her face didn't have an expression.

"So what did the note say?" asked Fiona.

But Sophie put up an elfin hand. "Wait a minute," she said. "Why are we even doing this note thing? Why don't we just talk about it at lunch?"

Kitty giggled. "Because, silly, Maggie—"

"Maggie wants to help, don't you, Mags?" Sophie said.

"How does this solve anything?" Fiona muttered to Sophie as they headed for the cafeteria behind Kitty and Maggie.

"I think Maggie's gonna tell us that herself," Sophie said. "I want to hear her idea about a stakeout."

Fiona twisted her lips. "I do too. Just when I was starting to really despise her, I have to agree with her."

Sophie linked her arm through Fiona's. This was more like it.

After they all put their lunches in the center of the table, Sophie said to Maggie, "So tell us your idea."

Fiona picked up a half of Sophie's PB&J. "This looks good. We never get this at our house."

Sophie flipped her braids over her shoulders. "All right, Nimbus. Please speak."

"I think we should have somebody in the space station all the time, keeping watch," Maggie said.

"All the time?" Kitty said. "Like, sleep up there?"

"No. All the time from two thirty in the afternoon until six and all day on the weekend."

"All four of us at once?" Fiona said.

"No. We take two-hour shifts, two of us at a time."

"Who goes with who?" Kitty said. She clearly had a fearful eye on Maggie.

Sophie looked at Fiona. She hadn't challenged Maggie's idea so far, which meant she actually thought it might work. But her nostrils, Sophie saw, were in the first stages of flaring.

"How should we choose partners?" Sophie said to her.

"I know," Kitty said. "We put our names on pieces of paper and whoever's name we pick is our partner."

They all looked at Kitty in surprise. After all, she usually wasn't the one coming up with the ideas.

"That's what my mom does with me and my sisters when we go anyplace. Everybody has to have a buddy."

Sophie nodded. That made sense. There were six girls in Kitty's family. They would all get sick of one another if they didn't switch off now and then.

"I'll write my and Kitty's and Maggie's names, and then Soph, you pick one." Fiona was already selecting a gel pen from the complete collection in her bag. "Whoever you pick is your partner, and then the other two go together."

"Roger," Sophie said quickly. And then she prayed she wouldn't pick Kitty, which would put Fiona and Maggie together. That could mean the end of the space station before the first hour of the stakeout was over.

She fished around in the Tupperware container Kitty's carrot sticks had been in and pulled out a slip of paper. *Nimbus*, Fiona had written.

Sophie tried not to look stunned. Two hours every day alone with Maggie from now until next week when they turned in their project? Maybe there was another way to do this.

But she held up the paper and said, "It's you and me, Nimbus."

Maggie broke into the biggest smile Sophie had ever seen on her face. A pang went straight through Sophie's chest again.

Well, God, she thought, *I guess that must be my job.*

She knew the first thing she was going to have to do in the space station that afternoon was keep Maggie from complaining the whole time that she didn't have any records to keep. Maybe now Sophie would be able to give her the idea she'd been trying to tell the Expedition Crew for two days, only either Fiona or Maggie kept cutting her off: Maggie could write down how long it took for the crew to assemble each part of the space station, which would be sometimes longer and sometimes shorter than it had taken the people in space. She hoped Mrs. Utley would just ignore the fact that the *Freedom 4* was lighter than the International Space Station, like by about a million pounds.

Hey, Sophie thought. *I really am doing my job.*

She just hoped God would do his.

Meanwhile, Maggie wrote up the schedule and had a copy for each of them by sixth period. Even Fiona had to admit it looked very scientific, although she did say to Sophie, "Since I live there, I could come up with you two and hang out."

Sophie got a sudden image of Fiona rolling her eyes at Maggie for two hours, until her eyeballs disappeared completely into her head. It wasn't pretty.

"No, Jupiter," Captain Stella Stratos said. "I know your loyalty to *Freedom 4* goes very deep, but I want you to be fresh for your own shift. You can't properly do surveillance if you're overtired."

"What?" Maggie said.

Sophie sighed. "It means we'll be just fine on our own," she said.

Maybe she could work on Maggie's imagination a little bit up in that tree house and she wouldn't be so bossy and Fiona would stop wishing she would disappear. One thing was for sure—this beat worrying about the Fruit Loops. Besides, if the Corn Flakes could get along and be strong, even the Fruit Loops couldn't drive them nuts.

By the time Sophie got the camera from Boppa that afternoon—because he was keeping it there for her so Mama didn't have to deliver it every day—and got up to the tree house, Maggie was already copying the information Fiona had given her onto one side of a page in a notebook. Sophie watched her while she munched on the Rice Krispies treats Kateesha had transported up to them.

She's really kind of pretty, Sophie thought, *in a scientific kind of way.*

Captain Stella Stratos sat back and watched the businesslike Nimbus work. She is so important to our crew, she thought. We wouldn't be able to achieve our goal without her. Captain Stella Stratos leaned closer to her loyal crew-woman to get a better view of her work. If you would only smile now and then, Stella wanted to say to her.

"Take some joy in saving the planet," Sophie said.

"We're not saving the planet," Maggie said. "We're doing a science project." She edged away from Sophie. "And how come you're practically in my lap?"

Sophie blinked. She was sitting so close to Maggie, they were barely taking up a whole place on the bench. She scooted back.

Maggie put her pencil down and blinked back at Sophie.

"What?" Sophie said. She was getting bristles under her collar. Fiona must feel like this times ten when she was around Maggie.

"We're just trying to keep somebody from tearing this thing apart," Maggie said. "You don't really think we're saving the planet, do you?"

Sophie shrugged.

"Well you don't, do you? This is a little puny science project. The universe goes out for millions of miles."

"Okay, no," Sophie said. She could hear her voice squeaking. "But it seems more real when you pretend."

"But it isn't real."

"But it seems like it."

"So?"

"So—it's fun."

Maggie picked the pencil back up and examined its point. "It's not fun for me," she said.

"Then why—" Sophie bit at her tongue. No, it wouldn't be the Corn Flake thing to ask Maggie why in the world she wanted to hang out with them then. Fiona, she knew, would have asked it in a heartbeat. "Why isn't it fun?" Sophie said.

To her surprise, Maggie's dark face was suddenly fringed in red, and she looked up at the wings and down at the space lockers and out at the robot arm—everywhere but at Sophie. "Because I'm not any good at it," she said finally.

Sophie didn't say anything. After all, Maggie was right about that. She'd just always thought Maggie wasn't even aware that she acted like their robotic arm in every scene they'd ever done for a film.

"Maybe you just haven't practiced enough lately," Sophie said. "How old were you when you stopped playing pretend?"

"I never started," Maggie said.

"Nuh-uh! Everybody plays pretend when they're little." Sophie grinned. "My parents get upset because I didn't ever grow out of it."

Maggie's face got smushy, like she was forgetting to do something with it that she always did to hold it in place. She said, "I wish—"

And then she stopped, and her face went tight and smooth again and she said, "I'm just not a pretending kind of person. My mother says life isn't a fairy tale. She says we all have to grow up sometime."

"Oh," Sophie said. "My mama never says that. She—"

And then it was Sophie's turn to stop. Maybe that was what was happening with Mama. She didn't believe in fairy tales anymore. Or playing. Or even laughing. Maybe Mama had grown up.

Sophie felt a wave of sadness that nearly knocked her sideways. Most of it seemed to land right on her chest.

"All right, Nimbus, back to work," said Captain Stella Stratos. She tried to make her voice crisp, like the people on the Discovery Channel. "I must continue to document our progress on film. Look scientific, would you?"

Maggie blinked at her and went back to copying. Captain Stella Stratos zoomed in for a close-up. The eyes that had never imagined herself as a unicorn or a princess or a world-famous astronaut went back and forth across the page like the blinking cursor on a computer screen.

I'm so sorry for her, thought Captain Stella. She has no place to go when she's afraid.

Then the captain sighed and closed her eyes and guided the space capsule through a whole shower of flying rocks.

"Don't be afraid, Nimbus!" she cried.

"I'm not," said Maggie.

But somehow Sophie knew she was.

Ten

Sophie decided that for the next two days when she was up in the tree house with Maggie, she was going to be Captain Stella Stratos the whole time. Then maybe Maggie would have to start using her imagination more.

The first day, Sophie tried being Captain Stella by herself the whole two hours. Maggie just logged in her information and stared at Sophie every few minutes—as if she were watching an elephant fly.

The second day, Friday, when they had the just-before-dark shift, Sophie peered through the aluminum-foil window and called out, "Meteor alert! Meteor alert!"

Maggie calmly told her that those were not meteors, they were pinecones being pelted at them from below by Izzy and Rory. Seconds later Kateesha appeared and whisked the whole meteor shower into time-out.

Next, as Sophie handed Maggie the granola bars Kateesha transported up to them in the basket, she said, "These are our dried space rations for the day."

Maggie said, "Those were five dollars for a box of fifty at Sam's Club." Then she added, "My mom makes her own."

"She does?" Sophie said. "My mama does too. Well, she used to—"

It was too sad to go there. Sophie picked up her camera.

"Be Nimbus," she said. "I need some footage of you walking around the space station, hanging on to things so you don't float away."

"I'm not gonna float away."

"Just PRETEND!" Sophie took a deep breath. "We're going to use it in the project," she said. "I need it for GATE points."

Maggie gave that a few seconds' thought, and then she stood up and moved woodenly around the space station, now and then putting a limp hand on an old doorknob turned into a gauge or a lever constructed from a toothbrush handle.

She looks like she's counting heads, Sophie thought. Fiona's eyes would be rolling right up into her brain by now.

"Is that enough?" Maggie said.

"Sure," Sophie said. Just as she was about to push the Off button, Maggie looked down at her feet.

"I can do this one thing," she said. "It's sort of like outer space."

"Do it," Sophie said.

Maggie put one foot behind her and rolled the toes back, and then did the same thing with the other foot, so that suddenly she looked like she didn't have any bones.

"What's that?" Sophie said. She zoomed the lens so she could get the full effect. Maggie was oozing backward, but it seemed as if neither foot ever left the ground.

"Moonwalk," Maggie said. "My mom taught me. We do it in the kitchen all the time."

"Show me how!" Sophie said. She set the camera on top of her locker box and hurried over to stand beside Maggie.

Maggie broke the steps down into slow ones so Sophie could imitate her. It took a couple of toe stubbings to get the hang of it, but within a few seconds they were both gliding around the space station like two astronauts strolling across the moon.

"Look at us!" Sophie said. "We're amazing."

"We could do it faster," Maggie said.

She sped up the steps, legs sliding like she was walking on glass. Sophie tried it and landed square on her buns, feet sprawled out in both directions.

"You fell," Maggie said.

"I did!"

"You can't fall in space. There's no gravity."

Sophie's eyes widened. Was this Maggie *pretending*?

If she wasn't, she was close enough. Being as fluid as she could with a splinter stuck in the seat of her sweatpants, Sophie got up and tried it again. Maggie watched her for a minute, and then her face slowly broke into a grin.

"What?" Sophie said. "What's funny?"

"You. You look like you're a windup toy. Y'know, like you get in a Happy Meal."

"No, I do not!" Sophie said. A giggle bubbled out with the words.

But Maggie nodded. "Yeah. You do." And then she actually laughed. It was a deep sound, and it made Sophie think of chocolate. She had to laugh with her.

"Uh-oh," Maggie said. She pointed a finger at Sophie's camera. "You left it on."

"My battery!" Sophie said. "My father is gonna have a fit."

She picked up the camera and looked in the viewfinder.

"Did you get us?" Maggie said.

Sophie nodded and moved the camera over so Maggie could watch with her. There they were, moonwalking all over the space station, complete with Maggie giving instructions and Sophie dropping on her behind.

Maggie let loose with her rich laugh again, and her shoulders shook so hard, she jerked Sophie's arm and almost sent the camera orbiting into outer space. Then suddenly she stopped.

"Hey," she said. "Am I always that bossy? Like I am on this film?"

Sophie gave her hair a chew. "You know how to do a lot of stuff," she said slowly.

"But I'm bossy," Maggie said. "Don't let my mom see that movie. She'll say I was being President of the World again." Maggie ducked her head, sending the splashy hair down to meet over her nose. "She hates when I do that."

"You and your mom have fun, huh?" Sophie said. "Moonwalking in the kitchen and stuff."

Maggie looked up, and she smiled a very soft smile. "She's like my best friend."

Later, when she was chewing a pencil over her math homework at home, Sophie went back to the picture in her mind of Maggie and her mother dancing in their kitchen, having fun. Every time she thought about it, she felt a sadness flicker through her. It wasn't sad that they had fun together. It was that Maggie's mother was her best friend. That Maggie didn't have one her own age at school.

I remember what that felt like when I first moved here, Sophie thought. *Everybody had a friend but me, until Fiona came.*

But who wanted to be Maggie's best friend? She had said herself she was bossy.

But she could also moonwalk. And she had a chocolate laugh. And she was way smart.

Three reasons why I like her, Sophie thought.

Fiona spent the night with Sophie Friday night. They sat in the middle of Sophie's room with some mini-pizzas from the microwave and the lights off and the covers draped over the headboard to make a tent where they could shine their flashlight. With Lacie and her friend Valerie playing Beyoncé on the stereo in Lacie's room and Zeke out in the hall pretending he was Spider-Man and trying to climb up Sophie's door, they had to seclude themselves if they were going to get any best-friend stuff done at all.

"So, Soph—is it awful?" Fiona said.

"Is what awful?"

"Being up in the space station with Nimbus?"

Sophie carefully licked some tomato sauce off her fingers. She knew Fiona wanted her to say it was absolutely heinous—

"It isn't awful," she said.

"But doesn't she boss you around?"

"Sometimes."

"How 'bout all the time?" Fiona peeled a piece of pepperoni off her pizza. "Once this project is over, I think we should just—"

"She taught me how to moonwalk," Sophie said.

Fiona stopped, pepperoni on her lips. "You mean that dance thing?"

"Yeah. It's so cool. I'll show you—"

"I've seen it." Fiona's gray eyes were looking stormy.

"I thought you said you agreed with her about the stakeout idea," Sophie said.

"A lot of good it's doing. Since she's the one we're staking out, you don't think she's going to break something else while we're up there, do you?"

Sophie put down her half-eaten piece of pizza.

"What?" Fiona said.

"I don't really think Maggie's the one who broke our robot arm."

"Oh—so now you're her best friend," Fiona said.

"No!" Sophie said. "You're my best friend."

Fiona slanted her eyes down toward the pizza, but Sophie could tell she wasn't seeing the cheese. "Am I your only best friend?" she said.

"You can only have one!" Sophie said. "Du-uh!"

"Yeah," Fiona said. "Well, sometimes people forget that. I've had it happen." Then she shrugged and held back her head and let a string of cheese drop into her mouth. "Okay—so let's talk about our film. You know all the kids are going to be totally astounded by it."

Sophie nodded, but her mind was twirling around other things.

She's scared I'll like Maggie more than her.

Should I stop getting to like Maggie so Fiona won't get all jealous?

What if I do like Maggie and Fiona stops being my friend?

Sophie looked at Fiona, who was opening their purple book. Her eyes were shimmering again, the way they always got when the two of them were planning something astounding. She was the made-especially-for-Sophie-LaCroix best friend.

But thinking about Maggie made her squirm. Maggie, who didn't have a special bud. Maggie, who was up to three reasons for being liked. Maggie, who was probably giving everything she had.

The next morning when she and Fiona were brushing their teeth together—with matching toothbrushes—Sophie made a silent decision.

Today the whole time we're up in the Freedom 4, *I'm going to find out more reasons to like Maggie. When I get up to ten—then Fiona will understand.*

When they climbed into Daddy's truck for him to take them to Fiona's, Zeke was already in his car seat in the crew cab.

"Z-Man's going with you," Daddy said as Sophie slid in beside him and let Fiona have the front seat. "He's going to hang out with Izzy and the Ror-meister while you're working."

"Where are you going?" Sophie said.

She thought she saw the crinkles around Daddy's eyes get deeper.

"Your mother and I are going on a date."

"But you're married," Fiona said.

"You don't think a husband and a wife can go on a date?"

Sophie thought about that. Basically, adults could do anything they wanted, so why not? Besides, this sounded good. Mama and Daddy going to a movie and holding hands in there and eating out of the same popcorn. People didn't go on dates if they were about to ... No, this had to be a very good thing.

"I'll watch Zeke and I'll even take care of him tonight if you guys want to go on a really long date," Sophie said.

Daddy broke into a grin. "Okay, who are you and what have you done with my kid?"

To her own surprise, Sophie got a tight feeling in her throat, like she was going to cry.

It's all I have to give, she thought. *It's like MY loaves and fishes. Daddy, don't laugh at me.*

The minute they got to Fiona's, Zeke leaped out of his car seat and crawled across Sophie before Daddy could get the door open. He took off to join Rory and Izzy, with Fiona on his heels toward off a puppy pile of three kids in puffy coats and with runny noses. It was definitely the coldest day they'd had the whole winter. Icy breath was puffing out of everyone's mouths.

"You sure you want to go up in that tree house today?" Daddy said to Sophie. "You're going to freeze your nose off."

He reached down and caught her nose gently between the knuckles of two fingers. "It's too cute for you to lose." Then he looked at her closely.

"Are you crying, Soph?" he said.

"I think so," she said. She blinked hard. "I just wanted to help."

Daddy put his hand on her cheek. It almost swallowed it up. "You do help," he said. "Just by being you."

Then he coughed and reached back into the truck. "If you're determined to go up there," he said, "you're going to need this." He pulled out a thermos. "Hot chocolate. They drink it in space. I have it on the best authority."

It made Sophie smile a damp smile.

Maggie was, of course, already up in the space station when Sophie climbed the ladder, trying to write down more stuff with her gloves on. She had a bright yellow scarf pulled over her nose and mouth.

Sophie pulled out the blanket she had stuffed into her backpack and wrapped up in it. Then she produced the thermos and dug in her locker for two cups.

"Maybe we should watch the station from inside the house," Sophie said as she poured. "It's way cold up here."

"I will not abandon the *Freedom 4* in her time of need," Maggie said.

Sophie almost poured the rest of the hot chocolate right over her hand. She sucked on the glove finger where it dripped some and tried not to stare at Maggie.

Reason Number Four: Maggie is loyal.

Maggie joined her and took a cup with steam curling up from it. As Sophie was blowing on hers, Maggie said, "I'm not trying to be the boss of you, but I think you did something you weren't supposed to."

"For real?" Sophie said.

"You left your camera up here yesterday."

Sophie spit the sip she'd just taken back into the cup.

"I put it in your locker when I got up here this morning. Are you gonna get in trouble?"

Maggie's eyebrows were scrunched up, like she was really worried.

"Only if it's broken," Sophie said. She squeezed her eyes shut. "I can't look. You check it."

"I already did. It works okay." Sophie opened her eyes to see Maggie nodding very seriously. "You're lucky it didn't rain last night."

"Please," Sophie said. "That would be so heinous."

She was about to take another sip of her hot chocolate when there was a scream so loud from the direction of Huntsville, they both abandoned their cups and got to the railing.

"They shouldn't be doing that," Maggie said, voice as calm and heavy as ever.

Sophie's was not. "No kidding!" she squeaked.

Rory was hauling a little red wagon across the lawn, bouncing it through the now-empty flower beds and nearly turning it over when he got to a walkway. Which was not good, since Izzy was in the wagon, holding on to Zeke. Sophie realized she had to hold on to him because he couldn't hold on for himself. He was wrapped up in enough rope to tie all three of them up. He was the one doing the screaming.

"Somebody's gonna get hurt," Maggie yelled down at them.

If Rory heard that, he ignored her. He careened the wagon around a curve in the walkway on two wheels, just missing Kateesha, who was coming at him with both arms out. She had to step off the walk to avoid being plowed over, but that didn't stop her from reaching into her coat pocket and pulling out something that she put in her mouth. A high-pitched whistle made Sophie put her hands over her ears. And it definitely brought Rory to a sneaker-screeching halt.

In minutes Kateesha had Zeke untied and she was dragging both Izzy and Rory toward the house by the backs of their collars.

"Captain Stella!" she called over her shoulder. "Could you take Zeke on board for a few minutes?"

"I'm not allowed to," Sophie called back to her.

But Kateesha was too busy telling Izzy and Rory how long their time-outs were going to be to hear her. Sophie looked down at her little brother, who was looking up at her with his eyes twice the size they usually were. He looked smaller than ever from outer space.

I can't just let him stand there and freeze to death, Sophie thought. *Mama will understand.*

Sophie tried not to think that maybe the new grown-up Mama wouldn't, and helped Maggie get the still-hollering Zeke up the ladder. While Maggie closed the hatch cover, Sophie poured enough hot chocolate into him to make him stop howling. Then he looked around, and his eyes started to shine.

"This is COOL!" he said.

"He shouldn't touch anything," Maggie said.

Zeke looked at Sophie. "Is she the boss of me?"

"She's the president of the whole world," Sophie said.

"Nuh-uh!" Zeke said. And then he peered at Maggie from under his knit cap and said, "Are you?"

"No," Maggie said. "I just act like I am."

Reason Number Five: Maggie didn't lie about herself.

Maggie smiled at Sophie like they had a secret. Sophie made that Reason Number Six.

"What's over here?" Zeke said. Instead of pointing, he got up to stomp across the hatch cover toward the robot arm.

And then suddenly, he was down again. There was a silence, the kind that always came when Zeke fell and he was deciding whether to cry or not. He evidently thought he needed to because the wail he sent up went right through Sophie.

The minute she got to him, she saw why. The hatch cover had split right down the middle, and Zeke's leg was wedged between the two halves. Sophie watched in horror as blood soaked into his jeans.

Eleven

Sophie thought the floor was breaking open under her too. And then she realized she was just sinking down to her knees, staring at the blood.

"Go get help!" she said. "He's hurt bad! He's bleeding all over the place!"

Maggie got down beside her and bent over Zeke. "Stop crying," she said to him.

Her voice was so calm it made Sophie want to scream louder.

"You have to answer some questions," Maggie said.

To Sophie's utter amazement, Zeke choked back his tears to a lower level. "Can you move your leg?"

"Nuh-uh. It's stuck."

Zeke puckered up again.

"Okay—how about the part that's hanging down?"

Sophie realized for the first time that his leg had gone all the way through and it was dangling from the knee down. Zeke swung it a little and then started yowling again. There was no quieting him this time.

"You go get help," Maggie said to Sophie. "I'm gonna cover him up with a blanket and stuff."

"I can't! He's on the hatch cover!"

103

Zeke's shrieks went way up into the atmosphere, and Maggie looked hard at Sophie and then at Zeke. Sophie bit her lip.

"It's okay, Z-Man," Sophie said to him. "I'll get help some other way."

She went to the railing and shouted for Kateesha, for Boppa, for anybody. It wasn't hard, since she wanted to scream anyway.

But her shivery shouts seemed to disappear with the puffs of frosty breath that blew from her mouth. Then Fiona burst out onto the deck, dragging Boppa behind her. Boppa ducked back into the house and came out with a cell phone in his hand. Fiona was already standing at the bottom of the ladder by then, staring up at Zeke's dangling leg. Sophie had never seen her best friend look so white and wide-eyed.

"He's bleeding!" Sophie called to her.

"Boppa's coming!"

Their two voices tangled up into one high-pitched knot. Maggie's voice was the only calm one.

"He's not going anywhere," she said.

Sophie looked over to see that Maggie had Zeke bundled up and lying down with his other leg up. Zeke was still crying, but he wasn't making a lot of noise. He was watching Maggie's face as she talked to him, and he was nodding. Sophie figured Maggie was telling him he would be fine — or else.

Boppa's bushy eyebrows looked jet black against his skin as he took in the board situation. He was pretty white-faced himself.

"Okay," he called up to Maggie and Sophie. "I'm going to get up there and pry the parts of the board apart. You two are going to take Zeke by the armpits and pull him back, very slowly."

"Very slowly," Sophie said. She could hardly hear her own voice.

"Just get him so his leg is clear of the hole and don't move him any other way."

Maggie looked at Sophie. "That's in case it's broken," she whispered.

"Okay, ready?" Boppa said.

Sophie half crawled over to Zeke and got behind him on one side. Maggie took the other, and Sophie could see her holding her breath.

"One, two, three," Boppa called. "Now!"

Sophie could hear the boards splitting apart, and she and Maggie gave Zeke one gentle tug. Sophie covered her eyes and waited.

"His leg's still in one piece," Maggie said. "All in one piece is good."

Boppa was there like Spider-Man himself, with Fiona crawling in after him. He knitted his eyebrows over Zeke's leg and nodded. Sophie decided Boppa nodding was good too.

"It's not as bad as it looks," he said. "I'm calling Fiona's mother."

Sophie and Fiona clung to each other like baby monkeys while they waited for Fiona's doctor mom to get there. Sophie watched as Maggie helped Boppa get Zeke in a position where he fell into a soft whimper instead of the screams that were shaking the pinecones out of the trees.

I don't know what number reason I'm on, Sophie thought. *I just know I like Maggie enough for anything.*

When Dr. Bunting got there, she said Zeke needed to go to the emergency room. Boppa got on the phone and called Mama and Daddy to tell them to meet them at the hospital.

That was when it hit Sophie like a blast of frozen air. Mama had told her never to take Zeke up in the tree house. She was going to be so upset—so disappointed, so mad—that this could be it. The final thing. Just when she'd started to be Mama again.

Even Captain Stella Stratos can't fix this one, Sophie thought. *Because it's all my fault.*

By the time Sophie, Boppa, and Dr. Bunting got Zeke to the hospital, Mama and Daddy were already there. Sophie felt like she could almost see through Mama's pale face.

Things went by in a blur. From what Sophie could tell, Zeke was being put in a room with curtains, Dr. Bunting was telling Mama he would barely feel a thing, and Daddy was leading Sophie down the hall for interrogation.

He squatted down in front of her so that their heads were the same level. She was afraid to look into his eyes, so she fixed hers on the third button down on his shirt.

"What happened, Soph?" he said.

"I don't know," she said to the button. "I told you I'd watch him, and I was. I was protecting him from Rory and Izzy—and I'm not dreaming, he really was in trouble—"

"Soph," Daddy said. "Take it easy. I'm running out of breath."

She looked at his face. His eyes were shiny, not angry.

"Just tell me what happened. One word at a time, okay?"

But Sophie couldn't seem to slow herself down. "Mama told me not to let him go up there, but I had to—Kateesha told me to and I couldn't just let him stand down there and be all frozen—but Mama's going to be so upset with me she'll really leave us now!"

Sophie sucked in some breath, and her eyes went back to Daddy's button. "Are they going to have to amputate?"

Suddenly Daddy's big arms were around her, pressing her glasses right next to the button. "No, Soph," he said. "He'll get a couple of stitches and a Tootsie Roll Pop and he'll be driving us all nuts again within the hour."

Sophie started to cry, big old sobs that soaked Daddy's shirt. He just let her bawl until the tears dried up. Then he held her out in front of him with both arms.

"Now listen to me," he said. "Mama isn't going anywhere. I don't know where you got that idea, but she's our mama and she's staying right here."

All Sophie could do was stare. It was all too much to store in her brain right now.

"We'll talk about that some more later," Daddy said. "But right now, I want you to try to focus with me, okay?"

Sophie nodded.

Daddy got his face very close to hers. "Do you have any idea who cut that board?"

"Cut it?" Sophie said. She could feel her eyes bulging. "You mean, like, on purpose?"

"Boppa says he's sure someone cut it with a saw so when somebody put weight on it, it would break."

Sophie went cold. Daddy watched her face.

"One thing I can count on from you, Soph," he said in a soft voice, "is that you're always honest."

Sophie riveted her eyes to the button again, but Daddy tilted her chin up. She had to look at him.

"I don't know who it was," she said. "Fiona will say she does, but I don't think so because I have five — no — six reasons why I like that person and I know she wouldn't do it."

"And that person is?"

"It wasn't me," a voice thudded from the doorway.

Sophie whirled around, slapping Daddy in the face with her braids. Maggie was there, and her mom was right behind her. Senora LaQuita looked like she wanted to smother somebody.

"Fiona already told her dad she thought I did it," Maggie said. "Only I didn't. The only time I've been up there is when I was with somebody."

Senora LaQuita took Maggie's shoulders and pulled her back against her. "My daughter doesn't lie," she said.

"Mine doesn't either," Daddy said, "so I guess that puts Maggie in the clear."

But Maggie pointed a finger at Sophie, and for once her voice wasn't heavy and strong. It sounded like it was going to break.

"You do too lie," she said. "You told Fiona you thought I did it, but you told your father you didn't, so you're lying to somebody."

Sophie could feel her mouth dropping open. "I didn't—"

"I don't lie!"

"Neither do I!"

"Okay, whoa," Daddy said, hands up. "That's something you two are going to have to figure out on your own." He glanced up at Senora LaQuita. "Unless you want to take it on."

The senora gave him an are-you-kidding look.

"Nobody here thinks you cut the board, Maggie," he said, "so the important thing is to find out who did." He looked back and forth from Sophie to Maggie. "Any other ideas?"

But Sophie's mind couldn't even turn in that direction. She was still watching Maggie, who was staring hard at the floor. There wasn't a chocolate laugh within miles.

Maggie, I didn't tell Fiona that! Sophie wanted to cry out.

And then another thought seized her. Why would Fiona say she had?

With the deepest pang in her chest yet, Sophie knew Maggie was telling the truth. It was her beloved Fiona who was lying.

"Why don't we all just think about it?" Daddy said. "We'll sort this out after we get the Z-Boy home." He put his big hand on Sophie's shoulder and looked at Maggie. "You two okay? No bumps and bruises?"

Sophie shook her head. Maggie still wouldn't look up.

"I want to thank you, Miss Maggie," Daddy said. "I understand you really kept your cool up there in the tree house. Good job."

Maggie finally lifted her head a little then. But she didn't smile. She didn't look at Sophie. She just thudded out, "You're welcome."

Sophie felt a thud of her own. It was her heart dropping.

Zeke got his stitches and his sucker and fell asleep in the truck on the way home. Sophie sat in the backseat with him, her mind reeling. Actually, it was Dr. Stella's mind that was reeling.

The Freedom 4 *has been sabotaged right under our noses, she thought. And now the crew is divided. How is this to be solved? How am I going to talk to Astronaut Jupiter in a scientific way—*

Sophie came back to herself with a supersonic jolt. Once again, Dr. Stella couldn't make it okay with her way of looking at things. There was nothing scientific about this at all. This was about a best friend. A best friend who lied.

This time Sophie closed her eyes and pictured Jesus—whose eyes were sad.

What do I do? she said to him in her mind.

He didn't answer. He never did in words. She tried to remember what Dr. Peter said. Ask the questions, go to the Bible, and then wait for the answers. But what could the loaves and fishes possibly have to do with this?

When Sophie got home and was passing through the kitchen, Lacie pulled her head out of the refrigerator and told her that Fiona had called and wanted Sophie to call back. Sophie squeezed her eyes shut.

Just this once, couldn't you give me the answer right NOW? she said to Jesus.

"What's the matter? Do you have a stomachache?" Lacie said.

"Sort of," Sophie said.

To her surprise, Lacie was nodding. "This has been a rough day. I'd be surprised if you didn't puke. I feel like I'm going to."

And then she turned to the door where Daddy was carrying in the still-conked-out Zeke. Sophie watched her, chin dropped, for a few seconds.

Did that just happen? she thought. *Was Lacie just actually nice to me?*

But there was no time to think about that much, because the doorbell rang. When Sophie opened the door, Fiona and Boppa were standing there. Sophie's heart took another thud.

"We brought your camera back," Boppa said. His caterpillar eyebrows were sunken over his eyes.

"Why?" Sophie said. "Aren't we still going to use it?"

Fiona let out a loud breath through her nose. The nostrils were at an all-time flare.

"Hey, Soph," Daddy said behind her. "You going to make everybody stand out in the cold?"

He ushered Boppa in and did the usual guy handshake thing. Sophie could only look at Fiona as they stood there by the door. She was fuming like Sophie had never seen her do before. Before Sophie could go back to Jesus one more time and beg for some words, Fiona grabbed her arm and dragged her to a spot by one of Mama's tall plants.

"You are not going to believe this," she said. "It's so heinous I can't even tell you."

"I need to tell YOU—" Sophie started to say.

But Fiona forged ahead. "They're having the tree house taken down."

Sophie could feel her face freeze. "The *Freedom 4*?" she said.

"Yes! My parents said it was too dangerous and even though Zeke didn't get hurt that bad they don't want anybody else getting injured so they're having somebody take the whole thing down Monday."

The nose breaths were coming hard and fast now.

"But what about the space station?" Sophie said.

"They're saving that. They said we could set it up in the garage."

"But the film isn't finished—"

"I know! I told them this was so unjust and that Maggie is the one who should be punished, not us. But they—"

Sophie stopped listening to her. Words were orbiting in her mind, but they weren't confusing anymore. She shook her head.

"What?" Fiona said.

"Maggie didn't do it, Fiona."

There was a short silence, and then Fiona said, "Of course she did."

"She said she didn't, and I believe her."

With an impatient hand, Fiona brushed back the leaves that were tickling the side of her face. "You believe her? Just

111

because she said so." The eyes rolled. "Sometimes you're just too trusting, Soph."

"You told Maggie that I didn't believe her."

"I thought you didn't."

"I told you I didn't think she broke the robot arm."

Fiona craned her neck forward. "But I thought after you said we were still best friends, you would think what I thought. We've always thought the same thing."

Slowly Sophie shook her head. Fiona took a step back.

"Then I guess we're not best friends after all," Fiona said.

"WHAT?"

"As soon as we're done with the space station," she said, "I think we should just not be best friends."

Twelve

✳ ⌂ ✺

Sophie couldn't breathe. She could barely get out her next words.

"Not be best friends?" she said.

"Uh-oh."

It was a soft voice, just on the other side of the tree. Sophie peeked through the leaves at Mama.

"Trouble, my loves?" she said.

"No," Fiona said.

"Yes," Sophie said. She looked at Fiona through a blur of tears. "You just said we weren't going to be best friends anymore."

"Wow," Mama said. "This sounds like something that needs to be discussed over some of that gingerbread I made this morning. Come on, follow me."

For a minute, Sophie forgot that Fiona was about to end the best friendship in the entire galaxy. Mama was talking. Mama was baking things. Was Daddy right? Was she really there to stay?

Still, Sophie felt a stab as Fiona sat herself on one of the snack-bar stools and looked the other way. It didn't look like her best friend was there to stay.

"Lemon sauce?" Mama said, ladle poised over a bowl.

Fiona shook her head. Sophie didn't even answer. Mama put the spoon down and folded her arms on the countertop facing them.

"The best thing to do is to talk this out," she said. "Obviously there's been a misunderstanding, and believe me, the only way out is to go through."

There was something sort of I-know-about-these-things in Mama's voice that made Sophie listen to her very carefully. Fiona still didn't turn her head, but she nodded a little.

"All right," Mama said. "Could you use a moderator?"

"What's that?" Sophie asked.

"It's somebody who talks for people when they aren't speaking to each other," Fiona said.

"You can be that," Sophie said.

Mama smiled her elfin smile. "Okay. Now, I understand that you, Fiona, think Maggie cut the board that Zeke fell through. And you, Sophie, don't think she did it."

"And Fiona told Maggie that I did think so," Sophie said.

"And she believes her instead of me so I can't be her best friend anymore."

"Do best friends have to agree on everything?"

Fiona looked at Mama as if she'd just arrived from another planet's space station. "Yes. How else can they be best friends?"

Mama cocked her head, curls brushing against the side of her face. Sophie was getting a full feeling in her throat. THIS was her mama.

"Do your mom and dad agree on everything?" she said to Fiona.

"Uh, how 'bout no?" Fiona said. "They had an argument this morning about where the new hot tub is going to go."

"Okay—does that mean they aren't best friends?"

Fiona gave her another you're-from-outer-space look. "Are parents supposed to be each other's best friends?"

"Oh, most definitely," Mama said. "And one of the things that makes them best friends is that they know how to disagree. And that's what you two have to figure out. How to keep liking each other even though you don't think alike every second."

There was a silence. *I'm already doing that*, Sophie thought.

"I just get petrified," Fiona said. Her voice was thick.

"Petrified of what?"

"Of Sophie not wanting to be my friend. I never had one before, not like her. I was so scared of her liking Maggie better than me, I watched them in the tree house through binoculars this morning. That's how I knew Zeke got hurt."

Tears were trickling down Fiona's golden cheeks. Sophie started to cry too.

"Sophie," Mama said. "Do you have any plans to stop being Fiona's friend?"

"No!" Sophie said.

"What would it take for you to stop being friends with Fiona?"

"I would never do that!" Sophie said. "Not unless she did something really heinous—like hurt somebody—"

"Speaking of which."

Sophie and Mama turned to see Daddy standing in the doorway. His face was solemn, like he had bad news. Sophie was pretty sure she'd had enough bad news to last her whole life.

"Speaking of hurting somebody?" Mama said.

Daddy nodded. "I think you should all come in here and see this."

They followed him into the family room, Fiona trailing along behind as if she didn't want to have to talk to Sophie. Sophie was trailing her heart behind her.

Daddy had the camera turned on, and it took a second for Sophie to realize he was showing what they'd done on their film so far. Not much was happening at the moment. There was only a view of the empty *Freedom 4*.

Daddy cocked one eyebrow at Sophie. "We'll talk later about why you left your camera up in the tree house running for an hour last night after you and Maggie left. But I think you're going to be glad you did it."

The film continued, still showing the floor of the station, murky in the darkness. And then there was a darker shadow, cast by the hatch cover coming up. And then a head. And a set of ears that stuck out from somebody's head.

"Is that Colton Messik?" Fiona said.

Sophie nodded and watched another figure struggle through the hole, breathing like a tractor. "And that's Eddie Wornom. I'd know that backside anywhere."

"Okay," Daddy said, "now who's this kid?"

Another figure hauled itself up through the opening, plunking something on the floor ahead of him. It was a short guy who moved like he was in charge. It was Tod Ravelli, grabbing what she could now see was a saw and hissing something to Eddie's bulky form. The hatch cover came down over the opening.

And then a tearing sound suddenly ripped from the film, as Tod's elbow appeared over and over.

"Mercy," Mama said. "He's cutting that board."

"And we've got it on film." Daddy turned to look at Fiona. "There's your scoundrel."

Fiona stared at the top of the coffee table, and Sophie could tell she was blinking back tears again.

Sophie sat up tall. "We can handle them, Daddy. We'll—"

But Daddy put up a hand. "Soph, this is way too serious. This isn't some schoolboy prank. It was done deliberately, and you need to let adults handle it."

Sophie sank back against the cushions. It was okay. Even Captain Stella Stratos would let the big commander do his job.

Boppa got on the phone with Tod's parents and there was a lot of, "Yes, I'm sure. Of course I'm certain. I would never make an accusation like this without being absolutely—Yes, I'll bring the film over."

Boppa and Daddy left, and after Mama made sure Sophie and Fiona weren't crying and scared, she went upstairs to check on Zeke. That left Sophie and Fiona sitting in the family room on opposite ends of the couch, acting like they didn't know each other. Sophie did feel like crying then.

And it wasn't because the Fruit Loops had something so bad against them that they had actually tried to hurt them. It was because Fiona was so far away.

I want to fix it—I hate this! But I don't have any words. Jesus isn't giving me the words!

Fiona was running her toes back and forth across the coffee table and hugging a sofa pillow and looking miserable.

I have to say SOMETHING, Sophie thought. And she opened her mouth and let out the only words she had.

"You were wrong about Maggie, but anybody could make a mistake. I did."

Fiona shook her head, still sliding her toes on the coffee table. "You're never wrong. You're just way better than I am."

"But I was wrong. I thought Nimbus was too bossy at first too." Sophie scooted closer to Fiona. "She's not so bad, Jupiter. She's smart. She does the moonwalk. She has a laugh like chocolate and she's loyal and she knows first aid and she knows she's bossy."

She could see Fiona swallowing.

"But she doesn't know way-cool words and she doesn't have the best imagination in the universe and she doesn't know how to be somebody's friend. But I'm teaching her that." It was Sophie's turn to swallow hard. "And then she'll find her own best friend."

Fiona looked at Sophie with very round eyes. "Then you're not gonna trade me for her?" she said.

"Best friends don't DO stuff like that!" Sophie said. "I guess I need to be teaching you too."

Fiona hugged the pillow tighter to her, and Sophie thought about Dr. Peter's window seat. She felt a little like Dr. Peter must feel sometimes. She even wrinkled her glasses up her nose.

"I'm sorry I lied to Maggie about you not believing her," Fiona said.

"Okay," Sophie said.

Fiona looked at her with agony in her eyes. "Are you sure you don't hate me?"

"I'm sure," Sophie said solemnly.

Fiona looked down at her toes. "I bet Maggie will hate me forever."

"You don't want her to?" Sophie said.

"No! But what do I do?"

"How 'bout we call her?"

"You call her for me," Fiona said.

Before Sophie even started shaking her head, Fiona was rolling her eyes. "Okay, okay, I'll call her—only you have to be right there with me."

"Hello!" Sophie said. "Of course!"

It actually was Sophie who got Maggie on the phone, because she knew she would probably hang up if she heard Fiona's voice first. She was pretty surprised she didn't do it when she heard Sophie's. As it was, Maggie's words were thudding harder than usual.

"I'm mad at you," she said to Sophie.

"I didn't tell Fiona I thought you cut the board," Sophie said. "And she wants to tell you that herself."

"Wants" might have been too strong a word. Fiona looked like she would rather have hit herself in the head with the receiver than talk into it.

But Sophie was proud of her. She took the phone and took a breath and spilled out an apology in that one big burst of air. And then she deflated like a bicycle tire as she listened to Maggie talk. Sophie got next to Fiona so they could share the earpiece.

"Okay—I guess I forgive you," Maggie said. "Only I don't see why you had to lie."

"Because I thought you were going to take Sophie away from me."

"Take her where?" Maggie said.

Fiona rolled her eyes at Sophie. "You know, become her best friend instead of me."

"Oh," Maggie said. "No, I never have best friends."

"There isn't any reason why we can't all be best friends," Sophie said as she crowded her mouth next to Fiona's. "You and me and Kitty."

Fiona looked like she suddenly had the stomach flu, but Sophie held up a wait-a-minute hand. "Fiona's my BEST best friend, but you and Kitty can be my other best friends and we can be yours and Kitty's."

Maggie didn't say anything for so long, Sophie wasn't sure she was still there. When she finally answered, she said, "Okay. I'll bring the costumes over tomorrow."

Fiona collapsed against the couch.

"We have to have a meeting tomorrow anyway," Sophie said. "We'll tell you what's happening with the *Freedom 4* then."

When she hung up, Fiona was laughing. And laughing. And laughing.

"What?" Sophie said.

"I don't know," she said. "I just feel like laughing."

Sophie kind of did too.

Boppa and Daddy came back before an hour was up, and once again they and Mama and Fiona and Sophie gathered in the family room. Mama brought out the gingerbread and sauce, but nobody ate it.

"Tod confessed," Daddy told them. "Under duress."

"What does that mean?" Sophie said.

"He didn't want to do it," Fiona said. "I could have told you that."

"What's going to happen to him?" Sophie said.

"I don't know, but his father assured me he'll take care of it and it will never happen again."

"I want to believe that," Boppa said. Even his eyebrows looked sad. "But to be on the safe side, Fiona, I want you to avoid those boys at all costs."

"Uh, hello," Fiona said. "I wouldn't go near them if you paid me."

"Me neither," Sophie said. It felt good to be agreeing with Fiona again.

"He doesn't take all the blame though," Boppa said. The lines in his face looked like they were about to laugh.

"So he told on Eddie and Colton, huh?" Fiona said. "Like we hadn't already seen them on the movie."

"It isn't them he was blaming," Boppa said. "It's your old pals—what do you call them? Cheerios?"

"The Corn Pops?" Fiona said. "No way!"

But Sophie was bobbing her head up and down. "Yes way! I saw Julia looking at them when they were trying to get the note off Mrs. Y.'s shoe the other day. You know, THAT look?"

Fiona nodded. "Oh yeah. I know."

Daddy blinked at both of them. "What just went on?"

"It's a best friend thing," Mama said. "Known only to girls."

"Oh," Daddy said. "That would explain it. So we told Tod if he wanted to turn them in for putting them up to it, that was their choice, but he was the one holding the saw."

"Does that mean we can't turn them in?" Fiona said.

Daddy shook his head. "All you have is what Tod said."

"Too bad," Fiona said. "I'd like to see them go down again."

And then she looked at Sophie. Sophie was shaking her head.

"Or not," Fiona said.

Mama sat down on the arm of the sofa and put her hand on Sophie's shoulder. "I am really concerned about all this bullying. From now on, I want you to tell us every time anything like this even gets started. This has gotten way out of hand."

"Mama's right," Daddy said.

Sophie nodded until her head hurt. The only thing better than she and Fiona agreeing was Mama and Daddy agreeing. It was the best thought of the day.

Later, when everyone was gone, Mama came into Sophie's room.

"Whatcha thinking about, Dream Girl?" she said. She sat down on Sophie's bed next to her. Sophie scooted closer.

"I was thinking about loaves and fishes," Sophie said.

"Okay," Mama said. She didn't sound the least bit surprised. "And why were you thinking about loaves and fishes?"

"I don't know. I was trying to figure out what to do about Fiona and I asked Jesus to help me and I even thought about the loaves and fishes story because Dr. Peter said it would help but it wasn't helping . . ." She stopped for a breath. "And then it worked out anyway."

"What did you do to get it to work out?" Mama said. She crossed her legs in front of her and began to unbraid Sophie's hair with her tiny Mama hands.

"I just said what was in my head." Sophie rolled her eyes. "It really wasn't eloquent at all. And it wasn't scientific, which is what I'm into now."

"I've been sort of out of the loop on that. We'll have to get caught up." Mama ran her fingers through Sophie's loosened braid and gently shook out the crimped-up hair. "I think I know how the loaves and fishes story worked for you—because it's worked the same for me."

Sophie turned her eyes to Mama without moving her head, since Mama was now working on the other braid. "Did Dr. Peter give you that assignment too?" she said.

"No," Mama said. "You just made me think of it. I know I haven't been myself lately and I'm sorry for that. I know it's been hard for you."

"I didn't fall down in my grades though!" Sophie said. "I'm still in GATE—and we'll make the space station amazing, even in the garage—"

Mama stopped unbraiding and closed her eyes for a tiny second. "I know, and I'm proud of you. But you had nothing to do with my being unhappy."

"Then why were you?"

"For a lot of reasons that I've talked to Daddy and Dr. Peter about," Mama said. "Daddy and I have worked out our tangles, and God and I have worked out mine."

She leaned across to the bedside table and picked up Sophie's brush. Sophie wriggled herself around and felt it run smoothly down the back of her hair.

"But when everything was in knots," Mama said, "I had trouble doing the things I needed to do."

"I know about that," Sophie said.

"Yes, you do. And I bet you know that when that happens, you can only give what you have, and God will fill in the rest until you really start listening to him again." Mama gave her soft laugh. "The answers are always there of course."

Sophie let her head fall back as Mama went on brushing.

"Mama?" she said.

"What, Dream Girl?" Mama said.

"Does that mean I don't have to fix everything? You know, like make everything okay for everybody?"

Mama stopped brushing, and Sophie could feel Mama's forehead pressing against the back of her hair.

"That's exactly what it means," Mama said. "All we have to do is love and act like we love. That's what Jesus does, right?"

Sophie closed her eyes right there and imagined herself in the hungry crowd. Only it wasn't on a hillside. It was in a school, and people were fighting and throwing things. Kind of like in Mrs. Y.'s class. She could picture Jesus standing up in the middle of all those kids and—not yelling—saying, "All right. Who has something that can quiet down all this racket and get everyone getting along?"

Sophie looked down at her hands. She wasn't holding anything. But she knew there was something she could give. Something she would always have with her.

I know there's a reason to like every person here, she told Jesus. *I've got a bajillion for Dr. Peter and a bunch for Fiona and I'm getting a big list for Maggie too. I'm even starting to like Lacie.* She took a whisper breath. *Anyway, that's all I have. If people could just look at the good reasons . . . That's all I have.*

Mama slid her arms around Sophie. "I don't know where you are right now, my Dream Girl," she said. "But wherever it is, I think it's a very good place to be."

It was a good place, Sophie decided when Mama was gone. She snuggled into the pillows. Now if she could only think of a reason to like the Corn Pops. That was a dream she'd save for tomorrow.

Glossary

advantageous (AD-van-tage-us) doing something that helps you, or someone else, out; something that gives an advantage

aeronautics (AIR-oh-nah-ticks) the science of flying airplanes and spaceships

amputate (AM-pew-tate) removing a someone's body part, like an arm or a leg

calculations (kal-kyu-LA-shuns) doing addition, subtraction, multiplication, division, or a mix of all, to get an answer

cease and desist (seese and de-SIST) a command that means to stop doing something immediately and not to do it again

clandestine (clan-DEHSS-tin) secret in a rather sneaky way

degradation (de-gre-DAY-shun) doing really nasty things that make someone feel bad about who they are

duress (der-RESS) pressure you feel to do something you don't want to do

endure (in-DUR) to get through and accept something that is happening

heinous (HAY-nuhss) shockingly mean, beyond rude, or really nasty

imbeciles (IM-buh-sulls) complete and total idiots

imperious (im-Pir-E-us) acting all snotty and stuck-up, like a spoiled empress

intergalactic (in-ter-ga-LAC-tick) a place in space that is somewhere between earth and really, really outer space

microgravity (my-crow-GRAV-i-tEE) when gravity becomes really weak and everything just floats around

moderator (mod-er-A-ter) someone who acts as a go-between when people are in huge fights; they keep things calm

nanosecond (NAH-no-sec-und) one-billionth of a second, or the time it takes for everything to go wrong

ozone (O-zone) the hazy layer around the earth that keeps us from frying up and getting really sunburned

pact (packt) a promise to do something, no matter what

sabotage (sa-bo-tahge) to cheat by purposely wrecking something someone else did so you can win

scathingly (sKAY-thing-lee) used negatively, it means really harsh and nasty; it can also mean *incredibly* when used positively, like "a scathingly great plan."

scintillating (Sin-till-ATE-ing) something that is so fun, interesting, and exciting that you just *have* to be a part of it

stratosphere (Stra-tuh-sfear) the highest point of the earth's atmosphere, or the last level of air on earth

Sophie Steps Up

One

❋ 🐦 ❋

Sophie LaCroix could not believe what she had just heard.

There was no way Miss Blythe had just announced that the sixth-grade class was going to get to do a performance showcase—on the stage—on a Saturday night—in front of a REAL AUDIENCE. And that the top three performing groups would each get a prize.

In Sophie's world, dreams like THAT just didn't come true every day.

Sophie's best friend, Fiona, grabbed her hand and squeezed it until Sophie's fingers looked like red lipsticks.

"Do you think she'll let us pick our own groups?" Kitty whispered on Sophie's other side. Her robin's-egg-blue eyes were nearly bulging, the way they always did when she was nervous. Which was a lot.

"She would be nonsensical not to," Fiona whispered back. "We're the Corn Flakes."

"So?" That came from their other friend, Maggie, whose voice thudded across the table they shared. "Teachers don't care about that."

Sophie looked at Miss Blythe, who had her back to them, writing dates and times and requirements on the board with squeaky chalk. She was their arts teacher, and Sophie had often thought she couldn't have been anything else.

Miss Blythe was tall and wore long skirts and bracelets that bounced with bright-colored charms. She swayed like a new tree when she walked, the strands of her waist-length blonde hair streaming down her back as if they were rays of sunlight. With her long fingers constantly punctuating her sentences in the air, Sophie had a hard time imagining her as a lawyer or a greeter down at Wal-Mart. And Sophie could imagine just about anything.

Is Miss Blythe the type to let friends—best friends who can't bear to be separated—work together? Sophie thought. *Or would she subject her students to pure torture at the hands of girls like the Corn Pops?* They'd only had arts class for about a month. It was hard to say.

"I can't work with Julia and them!" Kitty was whining. She did that a lot too. "She and B.J. and Anne-Stuart and Willoughby—they would be so mean to me!"

"Yeah, they would torture you," Maggie said in her usual flat, factual voice. "Any of us."

Sophie could tell by the way Kitty was whimpering that none of that was making her feel any better. It wasn't doing much for Sophie either, for that matter. She shook her acorn-colored hair off her shoulders and adjusted her glasses as she leaned into the table. The rest of the Corn Flakes leaned in with her.

"We just have to pray really hard," she said. "We have to squeeze our eyes shut and whisper to God in our heads."

"That'll look weird," Maggie said. Sophie saw that she was on the point of rolling her very dark eyes. Maggie was Cuban, so everything on her was dark except her extra-white teeth.

"Corn Flakes are weird," Fiona told her. "That's what makes us unique. Close your eyes."

They all did, clutching each other's hands under the table. Just before she shut hers, Sophie saw the Corn Pops clinging to each other too, but she was pretty sure they weren't praying.

In fact, Sophie wondered if the Corn Pops EVER prayed. What they did do, as far as Sophie could tell, was think they were better than everybody else because they had more money than rock stars and could get their way no matter what. "No matter what" included cheating, lying, gossiping, and teasing people about anything they thought was too weird.

And since the Corn Pops considered everything the Corn Flakes did way too weird, Sophie and Maggie and Kitty and Fiona were their favorite targets.

At least we used to be, Sophie thought now. *Until they got in so much trouble for doing bad stuff and blaming it on us.*

It was a little bit of a comfort that the Corn Pops wouldn't dare do anything else to the Corn Flakes, at least not anything they could possibly get caught at. But Sophie knew the Pops had ways of getting away with things that could escape even the really smart teachers. She sure hoped Miss Blythe knew a Pop from a Flake and wouldn't try to mix them together.

It's pretty easy to see the differences, Sophie thought.

The Corn Pops only wanted to be popular—which was why they were Pops—and they would do anything to stay the boss of everybody else in the sixth grade at Great Marsh Elementary, which was where the corn part came from. Sometimes they were so corny in the stuff they did.

Sophie unsquinted her eyes open a little so she could peek at her fellow Flakes. Fiona, with her rich-brown bob that fell over one of her gray eyes. Maggie, so serious and stocky and practical. And Kitty, with her curly ponytail and her little nose that looked like it was made of china.

Corn Flakes are corny too, Sophie thought. *That's what everyone says just because we like to make up stories and make films out of them, and we don't care what anybody else thinks about that.*

Once, back when Kitty was still a Pop, the CPs had said Sophie and Fiona were a couple of "flakes." It was so perfect it had to be their name. After that, the girls who were all into sports were the Wheaties and most of the boys were Fruit Loops. The best part was that all the group names were a secret among the Corn Flakes.

"If everyone is awake, I'll finish explaining the project," Miss Blythe said.

Sophie's brown eyes sprang open, even though she hadn't actually gotten to praying at all. She pulled her elf-like body up as tall as she could in her chair. It wouldn't be good to be caught daydreaming, or Daddy would take her video camera away from her, and Corn Flakes Productions would be no more. That was the deal with her father—stay out of trouble and make nothing less than a B in school and she could keep the camera. Mess up and it was all history.

"I want at least four people to a group," Miss Blythe said. "And I feel very good about letting you choose your own—"

The rest was drowned out by shrieks that bounced off the walls and back again. Even as Sophie was hugging Fiona and hoping Kitty wasn't going to spill off her chair into a puddle of relief, she saw that the Corn Pops were every bit as excited. B.J.—the pudgy-faced one with the swingy blonde hair—was whistling through her teeth. Willoughby, of course, was letting out one of her poodle laughs that could set a person's fillings on edge, and Anne-Stuart was blowing her nose. Anne-Stuart had sinus issues. She was always blowing her nose.

Above it all was the Corn Pop Queen Bee, Julia Cummings, tossing her thick, curly auburn hair back from her face and looking as if she had expected nothing else. After all, she always got what she wanted.

Even as Sophie watched her, Julia turned to meet her eyes. Julia's went into slits, but she wore a smile that looked as if she'd selected it from a rack of grins and stuck it onto her face. Sophie had learned that every one of Julia's smiles had a message to send. This one clearly said, *Thank heaven I didn't get stuck with any of you.*

Sophie smiled back—a real smile. People always told her that her smile was wispy, like a wood fairy's. Sophie didn't know about that—she just knew that right now, it wiped Julia's own grin right off her mouth and replaced it with another message, etched into a sneer:

Don't even think about getting a prize, Sophie LaCroix, because we are so going to win.

"All right—let's settle down," Miss Blythe called out above the din. "Artists are disciplined people—remember that."

She perched on the high stool at the front of the room and began to make periods and commas in the air with her long fingers as she talked.

"Each group must decide on an idea for a performance that is to last no more than ten minutes at the very most."

One of the Wheaties, a softball-playing girl named Harley, poked her arm into the air. "What kinda stuff can we do?" she said. Her group all had their foreheads in twists, Sophie noticed.

"Anything the audience might enjoy," Miss Blythe said. Her eyes took on a dreamy look. "You can sing, dance, do gymnastics, present a poem—"

That got a couple of snickers from some of the Fruit Loops, but Miss Blythe ignored them.

"Think about what gifts and talents the members of your group have and put them together into something fabulous. And remember ..." She arched an eyebrow at the class. "You will be graded not only on the performance itself, but also on how organized you are and how well you are able to work together."

Sophie sighed happily. Maggie would be in charge of organization. Maggie, herself, and Fiona would do the thinking. And Kitty would do whatever they wanted her to because she always did.

"We are so going to have the best one," Fiona whispered to them.

"I want you to meet with your groups now," Miss Blythe said, curving a comma with her pinkie finger, "and go to work on coming up with an idea. I need to see it in writing by one week from today. That's next Thursday. If you don't have anything by then, I will assign a poem for your group to present."

"She'll have ours way before next Thursday," Maggie said.

As soon as Miss Blythe punched out the final period with a deep-purple fingernail, Maggie got out the Corn Flakes' purple Treasure Book and the special color-of-the-day gel pen, a shade of pale peach. Fiona got her finger around the section of hair that hung over her eye and twirled it. Sophie recognized that as her creative thinking pose. Sophie's was to tuck her way-skinny legs up under her and gaze at the ceiling.

It was Kitty, however, who spoke first. "Good thing we already know what our talent is. What can we make a film of?"

"Film?"

They all looked up at Miss Blythe, who had stopped beside their table with a swish of her lavender skirt.

"That's what we do," Fiona told her. "We write scripts and make films out of them. They're always educational. We do our research and we have costumes and—"

"I'm impressed," Miss Blythe said. "But you can't make a film for the Sixth Grade Showcase. This has to be a live performance."

Then she looked at the Corn Flakes as if they obviously didn't know what art really was and swept off to visit the Wheaties.

Kitty's voice immediately spiraled up into a whine. "But what do we do if we can't make a film?"

"Not fair," Maggie said.

"I'm gonna go talk to her," Fiona said.

But Sophie shook her head. "We'll think of something else," she said. "I get in trouble when I argue with teachers."

Fiona plucked at her little bunch of a mouth with her fingers. "Let's go around the table and everybody say what their talent is—besides making films."

For a long moment, nobody said anything. Finally Fiona snapped her fingers.

"I used to take ballet," she said.

"When?" Maggie said.

"When I was five. Only my parents had to take me out because the teacher didn't like me. I kept correcting the way she was pronouncing the positions. She was saying everything wrong."

Maggie had the peach pen poised over the blank page. "So Fiona can dance, but I can't."

"Me neither," Sophie said.

Kitty shook her head.

"Next," Maggie said. "I can make costumes, period."

"And you're the best at it," Sophie said. "Whatever we decide to do, you get to make them for us."

Maggie jotted that down and then looked at Kitty.

"Me?" Kitty said. "I can play the piano. Except the only song I know is 'You Ain't Nothin' But a Hound Dog.' My grandma taught me it. She says it's a classic."

"You know my talent," Sophie said. "I imagine things."

"So what are you imagining right now, Soph?" Fiona said.

"Oh no," Kitty whispered suddenly.

Sophie followed with her eyes to where Kitty was pointing. All the Corn Pops were squealing up to Miss Blythe's desk, and Anne-Stuart was waving around a piece of paper, which she floated down in front of Miss B.

"They couldn't have their idea written up already," Maggie said. She glanced at the wall clock. "It's impossible."

Fiona narrowed her eyes into little points. "They probably cheated."

"Class!" Miss Blythe said. She shot her index finger up into an exclamation point. "Julia's group has already come up with a marvelous idea! They are going to perform a dance with costumes. Doesn't that sound fabulous?"

"Fabulous," said some Fruit Loop in a bored voice.

"Okay, Flakes," Fiona hissed between her teeth. "Everybody has to come up with at least one idea by tomorrow morning—even if it's lame."

Maggie wrote that down too.

"I know your idea won't just be average brilliant," Fiona said to Sophie. "Yours will be scathingly brilliant."

"Oh, by the way—"

That was Anne-Stuart's voice, coming out of her always-stuffy nose. "We are going to need one more dancer. If you are interested in being in our spectacular production, see me and we will set up an audition for you."

Sophie pulled her Corn Flakes in around her with a spread of her arms.

"I'm glad none of us can dance," she said. "Because we will always stick together, right?"

They all agreed that they would. Always.

TWO

Sophie could hardly keep her mind on math and science in Mrs. Utley's classes that afternoon, and for once it wasn't because she was imagining herself as Antoinette the French heroine, or Dr. Demetria Diggerty the archaeologist, or Astronaut Stella Stratos. All she could think about was what on earth the Corn Flakes were going to do with one under-trained ballerina and a piano player who could only clunk out some old song about a dog.

She was trying to picture how they could get Fiona's talent for using big words in there when she heard Fiona coughing.

That was the signal that Sophie was in danger of being caught flitting into Sophie World instead of multiplying numbers with decimals. When she looked up, Fiona was jerking her head toward the Corn Pops.

They had their math books open, but their pencils were scrawling out the notes they were passing to each other.

Probably more ideas for their "spectacular dance," Sophie thought. *I'm really glad I'm going to see Dr. Peter today. I know he can help.*

Dr. Peter was Sophie's therapist—her sister, Lacie, still said he was her psychiatrist, even though he wasn't—and one of her favorite people in the galaxy. He was the one who had made it so she could have her camera and make better grades and have real friends. If it weren't for him, Sophie knew she would still be thinking Daddy didn't love her as much as he did Lacie and Zeke.

Mama was in front of the school in the Suburban to pick her up after her last class and take her to Hampton, where Dr. Peter had his office. As usual, Sophie's five-year-old brother, Zeke, was in the backseat yacking his head off.

"I liked it better when we went to Dr. Peter every week," he said to Sophie, instead of hello.

"We?" Mama said. She gave Sophie her gentle grin, which Sophie always figured was a lot like her own. Mama was small and elfish like her too, and her hair would be brown if she didn't streak it so it caught the light. "You never had a session with Dr. Peter, Zeke!"

"He's talking about the ice cream," Sophie said. "He knows you'll take him to Dairy Queen while you're waiting for me."

"Only now it's way too long between times," Zeke said. He puckered his forehead so that he looked like a miniature of Daddy. Except Daddy didn't wear his dark hair sticking up everywhere.

"Two weeks is not a long time," Mama said to him.

Sometimes it is, Sophie thought. Even back when they had first switched from twice a week to once a week, Sophie had felt like it was forever from one Dr. Peter visit to another. Now that she went only twice a month, she could store up so many things to talk to him about there was hardly time to spill it all out in the one hour they had.

But today I'm gonna talk about one thing, she told herself as Mama pulled up to the building, *and that's the showcase.*

As always, Dr. Peter was waiting for her at the front counter with his blue eyes twinkling behind his glasses and his mouth in a watermelon slice of a smile. Sophie loved those things about him—and the short, curly hair stiff with gel, and the faded freckles that danced on his face. She also liked it that he wasn't as tall as a lot of adults, especially Daddy, who towered over everybody. Daddy was getting better about not looking down at her, but Dr. Peter never had.

"Your shirt has four-leaf clovers on it!" Sophie said as she followed him back to the room where they always talked.

"St. Patrick's Day isn't far away," he said. "I'll be celebrating it all month."

"Why?" Sophie said. She settled herself on the window seat and selected one of the pillows shaped like a face. She always tried to pick one that had an expression to match what she was feeling. With the one wearing stern eyebrows and a straight yarn mouth firmly in her arms, she was ready.

"Because I'm Irish," Dr. Peter said. "And proud of it." He popped his eyes at Sophie. "Don't tell me you don't like corned beef and cabbage!"

"Yucko-poohy!" Sophie said. "No offense."

"None taken. Now ..." He nodded at the pillow. "Do you want to tell me why you chose Mr. Determined to hold today?"

"Because I AM determined," Sophie said. "Do you want me to tell you why?"

Dr. Peter grinned. "Do I have a choice?"

Sophie plunged into the story, using different voices for the Flakes and the Pops and Miss Blythe, complete with her finger-making commas and question marks in the air. When she was finished she was out of breath. So was Dr. Peter.

"Whew!" he said. "That was some fast storytelling."

"I wanted plenty of time for us to discuss what I'm going to do," Sophie said.

Dr. Peter peered over the top of his glasses. Sophie did the same back with hers.

"What YOU are going to do?" he said. "Don't all the Corn Flakes have to decide?"

"We all have to agree," Sophie said. "But they expect me to come up with the best ideas because—well, that's the way it always is." She shrugged. "I'm not smarter—I've just had more practice thinking things up. And besides, I have to keep everybody from fighting. You know how they are."

Dr. Peter nodded soberly. Sophie had told him all about the problems the Corn Flakes had had in the past with Maggie being bossy and Kitty being afraid of her and Fiona being jealous of her because Sophie had gotten to like Maggie. It was Dr. Peter who had helped her figure out what the Corn Flakes Girls Guidelines should be. Things like no eye rolling.

"What's the worst that can happen if you don't come up with a brilliant idea for the group?" Dr. Peter said.

"Miss Blythe will give us some lame poem to recite and everybody will laugh at us and we'll get a bad grade and my father will take away my camera and there won't be any more Corn Flakes Productions and the Corn Pops will win and they will throw it smack-dab into our faces for the rest of our lives!"

Dr. Peter blinked at her behind his glasses. "All right then," he said. "I guess I'd better give you some help."

Sophie let out a relief sigh that came all the way from her heels, and she sank back into the pile of pillows. Dr. Peter pulled out his Bible, the one in the case with the frog on it. That was where the answers always were.

"How about a Jesus story?" he said.

"How about yes!"

"Now tell me again why we do this."

Sophie sat up straighter. "I can get to know Jesus better if I imagine him better, so then I'll know what to ask him and I'll know if the answer I think I'm getting later is really from him."

"You're amazing," Dr. Peter said. "I'm going to write down where the story is in the gospel for you to read later, because I want us to have time to talk about something else."

Sophie settled herself more comfortably while Dr. Peter wrote on a sticky note shaped like a shamrock.

"There you go. It's going to be a piece of corned beef for you to figure this one out."

"Don't you mean a piece of cake?" Sophie said.

"Nae, wee lass!" he cried in an accent Sophie had once heard from a policeman on an old Bugs Bunny cartoon. "It's corned beef I mean and so it is! In any case—you'll figure it out in the wink of an eye."

"And I'll report back to you in two weeks." Sophie tried to say it with the accent, but it came out sounding more like Bugs Bunny himself than the policeman.

"Ah—that's what I need to talk about." Dr. Peter rubbed his hand across his lips like he was erasing his Irish accent. When he spoke again it was in his real voice, the soft version. "You are doing so well, my friend," he said. "I wonder if you might like to try seeing me just once a month now."

No! Sophie wanted to shout. *No—I need you! How will I ever—*

"You've learned so much," Dr. Peter went on, "and you've come in week after week telling me all the ways you're using everything you've learned. Pretty soon you're going to be taking on clients of your own."

"But I still need you!" Sophie said. "Don't I?"

"Do you?" Dr. Peter said. "Think about it."

"I guess I know how to do my best in school now," she said slowly. "And I get along with my dad."

"Those are big. And do you need me to help you keep doing those things? Aren't you doing them on your own now?"

Sophie pulled a strand of hair under her nose, like a mustache. "I am," she said finally.

"Then be proud of yourself! I even have a reward for you."

Dr. Peter reached into a basket on the floor and pulled out two huge green top hats, which he popped onto their heads. Sophie's hung down over her eyes.

"Ah, you have a bit of the Irish now, you do!" he said.

Sophie let a silvery giggle escape from her throat, but then she wilted again.

"Talk to me," Dr. Peter said. His face beneath the hat's brim was serious and kind.

"I'm afraid," Sophie said. "What if I start messing up again?"

"I'll be right here if you need me."

"But how will I know if I really need you?"

"You mean, what would be the signs?"

She pumped her head up and down.

"Okay—one ..." He pulled up a stuffed finger on a pillow. "If you find yourself escaping into one of your characters when you shouldn't be—like in school or when your dad is talking to you—and you're doing it to hide from something painful, that would be a sign."

"Then I could ask Mama to call you for a session?"

"If—and this is number two." Dr. Peter lifted another puffy finger. "If your parents can't help you with whatever is bothering you that makes you want to escape into Antoinette or someone."

Sophie could feel her eyebrows pulling together.

"You can trust them, Sophie-Lophie-Loodle," he said.

At the sound of his nickname for her, Sophie thought she was going to cry. That was okay in Dr. Peter's office, but she still blinked back the tears.

"They've learned a lot from their sessions with me too," Dr. Peter said. "And they've already proved that they understand you better."

"I know," Sophie said. "But I'll miss you."

The tears did come then, and she let them stream down her face. Dr. Peter had always told her tears would help her wash away things that hurt.

"I'll miss you too, Loodle," he said. "But I'm still going to see you every month for as long as you need me."

"Promise?" she said.

Dr. Peter's face got soft and mushy. "I promise. I'll try not to let you down."

And because he said that, Sophie was able to feel a little bit proud. She decided that was going to be her high at the dinner table that night.

Every evening at supper lately, Daddy asked everyone to tell their high for the day and their low—the best thing that happened and the worst. Sophie was pretty sure he had learned that from Dr. Peter.

"My high is that I get to go on my first youth group retreat this weekend," Lacie burst out that night almost before they had said "Amen" to the blessing. "And my low is that I don't have anything to wear. Mama, could we please go to the mall?"

Lacie didn't look at Mama when she said it, but at Daddy.

Here we go, Sophie thought. *Lacie thinks she can get Daddy to do anything she wants him to.*

Of course, it seemed to her that it kind of made sense, since Lacie was so much like Daddy. She had his dark hair and his height—she was tall for a thirteen-year-old girl. And she played every sport in the world, just like he always had, and she made straight As—which Daddy still would if they gave grades at NASA, the space center where he was a scientist. Besides that, Lacie and Daddy were both organized and practical and didn't understand that much about being creative, not as far as Sophie could tell. What was creative about shooting a basketball into a hoop until even your hair was sweating?

"How much is this going to cost me?" Daddy said to Lacie.

"Nothing," Mama said. "She has more clothes than Dillard's as it is."

"Dillard's has an apostrophe," Zeke said.

While Mama and Daddy and Lacie all went nuts over how intelligent Zeke was, Sophie got herself geared up to deliver her high and low. She had an idea that just might work.

But Zeke got to go next because he was suddenly the child genius.

"High," he said. "I got banilla ice cream dipped in choc-lit at Dairy Queen."

Lacie gave a snort. "You can say 'apostrophe' but you can't pronounce 'vanilla'?"

"What was your low, Z?" Mama said.

Zeke frowned, his dark little eyebrows trying to hood his eyes. "I gotta wait a whole month before I get another one, because Sophie isn't going back to Dr. Peter 'til then."

"He just took my high!" Sophie said.

"But congratulations, Soph!" Daddy said. He gave a grin that was as big and square as his shoulders. "Go, girl."

"We're proud of you," Mama said.

Lacie surveyed Sophie as she swirled her fork through her veggie stir-fry. "Then how come you're still weird?" she said.

Daddy made a loud buzzing sound, which meant Lacie was not playing by team rules.

"I also had a low," Sophie said.

"Is it the same as your high?" Lacie said. "You totally have a crush on the guy."

No, Sophie wanted to say. *You are my low.* But instead she told them about the showcase and how Miss Blythe wouldn't let the Corn Flakes make a film.

"Bummer," Daddy said.

"It's a total suppression of our creative gifts!" Sophie said, Fiona-like.

Lacie looked at Daddy. "What did she just say?"

"So, Daddy," Sophie said, "could you and Mama please talk to Miss Blythe and tell her that we're really good at making films and they aren't lame—"

Lacie grunted.

"—and it's what we're going to do our whole lives so we should be allowed to—"

She stopped, because Daddy was pointing his fork at her. "Nice try, Soph," he said. "But it sounds like Miss Blythe knows what she's doing. I'm sure you and your crowd can come up with something else."

"I told you that you would be more well-rounded," Lacie said to her, "if you didn't spend all your time pretending you're Hannah Montana or somebody."

"Lacie," Mama said, "did you miss the part where Sophie already has a mother?"

Any other time, Sophie would have taken a minute to enjoy the fact that for once Lacie was the one getting in trouble. But right now she was staring at Daddy, watching her great idea dissolve in the discussion-over look on his face.

"Do you want to brainstorm together?" Mama said to Sophie.

Sophie shook her head.

She was missing Dr. Peter already.

Three

When Sophie got to school the next morning, she headed for the cafeteria. That was where the Corn Flakes met before classes when it was bad weather or they had something very private to discuss. It was their secret planning place — on the stage behind the closed curtains, way back in the corner where scenery from past performances lurked in the darkness.

As Sophie slipped behind the curtain, which was more dust than velvet, she spotted the shadowy Corn Flakes hunched together on hay bales left over from the second grade's Barnyard Showcase. She felt like she was wearing cement shoes as she trudged toward them, because she didn't have a scathingly brilliant idea. She didn't even have a lame one.

Maggie already had the Corn Flakes' Treasure Book out, as well as the peach gel pen. She definitely hadn't used up all its ink at their last meeting.

"Here's what I'm thinking," Fiona said before Sophie could even find a spot to sit on a bale of hay. "We should have our own auditions. We can each present our idea like we're performing it. That way we really see what it could look like."

Maggie wrote that down in neat, steady cursive, while Kitty's voice spiraled up into a whine Sophie was sure only dogs could hear.

"I don't know how to do that!" she said. "You're making it hard, Fiona."

Sophie could tell Fiona wanted to roll her eyes, but it was a Corn Flake rule that they weren't allowed to make each other—or anybody else—feel like they were dumb.

Kitty gave a nervous giggle. "Okay—well—mine's a thing my sisters and I used to do—"

"Show us," Fiona said.

"Okay—one of us sits on a chair like we're getting our hair fixed so whoever it is has a sheet on—only your hands are tied behind your back ..." She demonstrated. "And then somebody else gets behind that person, but under the sheet with only their arms sticking out—"

She fumbled with her arms for a minute and then directed Fiona to get behind her.

"So Fiona's the arms and you're everything else," Sophie said.

"Right, and then one of us that's left tells the girl in front to do different stuff like put on lipstick or comb her hair." Kitty's words were now coming out in giggle-bubbles. "Only it's the one behind with arms that does it, so—"

"Tell us to do something," Fiona said.

"Get down so you can't see what you're doing," Kitty said. "That's the best part."

Kitty was giggling so hard, Sophie had to laugh herself. "Brush your teeth," Sophie said.

"She doesn't have a toothbrush," Maggie said.

"Pretend."

Fiona grabbed an imaginary toothbrush and went after Kitty's teeth, landing halfway up her nostrils. Kitty let out a shriek.

"Pick your nose," Maggie said.

"No!" Kitty cried—but she leaned her face forward to poke out the little china-nose, and Fiona stuck a finger right into Kitty's ear.

Even Maggie was laughing now—a chuckle that came from somewhere down deep. "Feed yourself a banana," she said.

"Wash your hands first!" Sophie said.

"Why?" said Fiona.

"Because you just picked your nose!"

Suddenly a shaft of light shot straight back to them from the front of the stage, and an all-too-familiar voice said, "Oh, sick!"

The light got wider as the curtains opened and B.J. came toward them, followed by Anne-Stuart, who was already sneezing from the curtain dust.

"You're picking your nose, Kitty?" Anne-Stuart said.

"No," Fiona said. "I'm picking it for her."

Somebody else shrieked. Sophie recognized that as Willoughby, who was obviously hauling the curtains open in the wing.

"I should have known," said Queen Julia as she sailed through the opening. She stopped in front of Kitty and Fiona, who were now in the act of eating an invisible banana that was going everywhere but into Kitty's wide-open mouth.

"Tell me this isn't your showcase presentation," she said.

B.J. shook her butter-blonde bob. "If it is, don't count on a prize."

"Did you ask if you could use the stage to practice?" Anne-Stuart said. She gave a juicy sniff. "We have permission to practice our dance—"

"Every day before school," B.J. put in.

"Oh, yes?" Fiona said. "Well, we—"

"We're just leaving!" Sophie grabbed her backpack and stared hard at the other Corn Flakes.

Fiona's eyes turned into dashes, but she said, "Right—only because we're fair—which is more than I can say for—"

"Let's get our stuff!" Sophie said.

Kitty giggled. "Get ours, Fiona."

Fiona's arms flailed around Kitty until Maggie put a backpack in each of her hands and Fiona and Kitty shuffled out still attached. Sophie was sure Kitty was going to need CPR, she was giggling so hard.

Whew, that was close, Sophie thought as she followed Fiona and Kitty to the steps. If Fiona had kept at it, it would've gotten way ugly.

That was another Corn Flake rule—no being evil to the Corn Pops, no matter how nasty they were being.

"Hey, Maggie," Julia called across the stage.

Maggie turned slowly around, peach gel pen behind her ear. "Me?" she said.

Sophie watched Julia select the I-want-something-from-you smile and paste it on.

"Did you think about what I asked you yesterday?" she said.

"Yeah," Maggie said. Her voice was heavy.

"So—are you going to make our costumes?"

"We really want you to, Miss Maggie," Anne-Stuart said. She was smiling too and nodding her head like that would automatically get Maggie to nod hers.

B.J. bobbed her bob. "You'll get a good grade if you work with us."

"Maggie's with us," Fiona said.

"We stick together," Kitty said. "We're the Cor—"

"Let's get to class!" Sophie heard her voice squeak, which it usually did when she was trying to save her friends from disaster. If the Pops ever knew they called themselves the Corn Flakes, they would practically have to move out of town.

"Can you believe they even had the nerve to ask Maggie that?" Fiona said to the Flakes as they hurried down the hall to language arts class.

Kitty looped her arm through Maggie's. "I would never let them take you away from us," she said.

Sophie was just forming a picture in her mind of Kitty hurling herself in front of Maggie like she was shielding her from an oncoming train, when Maggie said, "We're not really going to do that arm thing for our performance, are we?"

They all stopped in front of the classroom door and Kitty, Maggie, and Fiona looked at Sophie.

"Well," Sophie said carefully. "It was a good idea—but it wasn't a brilliant one. I know the Corn Flakes are capable of doing something really fabulous!"

She didn't have a chance to see how Kitty and Fiona were taking that because Mr. Denton called to them as he came toward them down the hall, leading a tall girl with reddish hair cut short and splashy.

"This is Darbie," Mr. Denton said. "She's joining our class."

The girl, who Sophie now saw from close up had dark eyes and smooth milky-white skin, didn't look to Sophie like she was "joining" anything. The way she seemed to be smelling at the air, it was more like she was starting her first day in a garbage dump.

I know how you feel, Sophie thought. *I despised being the new girl too. Hardly anybody even knew I was here until Fiona came.*

"Hi," Fiona said. "Where'd you move from?"

"Northern Ireland," Darbie said.

Sophie felt her eyes widen. "Ireland!"

"The real Ireland?" Kitty said.

"No, silly, the fake one," Fiona said. She smiled at Darbie again. "She doesn't get out that much."

"What's it like there?" Maggie said.

"Are there really leprechauns?" Kitty said.

Darbie didn't answer.

"Ladies—you sound like a bevy of reporters." Mr. Denton gave them his dial-tone-dry look. "Let's get Darbie settled in before we start interrogating her."

"I'm Kitty!" Kitty said as Mr. Denton led Darbie into the classroom.

"I'm Fiona—she's Maggie," Fiona said.

Even after they got into the classroom, Sophie didn't introduce herself because Darbie didn't appear to be listening, not the way she took herself to the other side of the room and stood with her back to them, straight and stiff-looking. Besides, an image was forming in Sophie's mind—of being from a foreign country and coming to an American school—*so proud of her homeland and yet so eager to belong. She was wearing a dress with green shamrocks on it, and a green derby—and carried a lunch box full of corned beef and cabbage—*

Okay, so she'd have to get Fiona to do some research on Ireland.

She tossed her hair in an Irish way—whatever that was—

"Hey, you—Soapy."

Sophie blinked into the face of Julia.

Just when she was getting to the good part. "What?" Sophie said.

"Who's the new girl?" Julia was wearing her we-really-are-friends-sometimes expression.

"Her name's Darbie," Sophie said. "She's from Ireland."

Julia looked almost impressed. "She dresses cute for being from a foreign country," she said. "Sometimes they dress funny."

"Those are all new clothes," Anne-Stuart said, sniffing as though she could smell their just-bought-ness.

"Old Navy," B.J. said.

Sophie edged away from the Corn Pops. It felt germy to be so close to them while they were sizing up Darbie from across the room.

"Go ask her if she wants to sit with us," Julia said to Willoughby.

Willoughby nodded her head of pecan-colored wavy hair and headed for the back of the room where Fiona was showing Darbie how to unlock her locker.

"I think she's sitting with us," Sophie said.

"She doesn't look weird at all," B.J. said. "She's more like us."

"Tell that Harley girl to move so Darbie can sit next to me," Julia said to B.J.

Sophie moved away, sure she had Corn-Pop-itis crawling all over her.

The Corn Flakes watched, mouths open, as Willoughby ushered Darbie to the seat B.J. had cleared for her, and Julia scooted her desk close to Darbie's, and Anne-Stuart provided her with gel pens, paper, and a container of lip gloss.

By lunch, Darbie was sitting at the Pops' table with a buffet in front of her that Julia had sent Willoughby through the line for with a wad of dollar bills.

At after-lunch free time, Julia and Anne-Stuart hustled Darbie off to a corner of the school yard, each with an arm around her. B.J. was walking backward in front of them and Willoughby trailed along behind, shrieking for no reason that Sophie could figure out.

"I guess she's going to be a Corn Pop," Kitty said as the Flakes lined up against the fence.

"Whether she wants to or not," Fiona said. "They haven't even given her a chance to talk to anybody else. That's so 'them.'"

"Hey," Maggie said, pointing a squared-off finger. "Look what they're doing."

Kitty squinted. "What ARE they doing?"

Sophie brushed away the hair the March wind tousled into her face. The Pops were now standing on the cement walkway along the fence, all in a row with Darbie in the middle. Everyone was watching Julia, who was moving like she was putting on an invisible pair of pantyhose.

"I know," Fiona said. "They're teaching her their dance."

"She's auditioning!" Kitty said.

Sure enough, as Sophie and the Flakes watched, Darbie imitated Julia—looking more like she was putting on overalls than nylons. The other Pops joined in, exaggerating their motions with Julia clapping her hands in rhythm and calling out, "One, two, three."

Suddenly, Darbie stopped and put up her hands.

"She hates it," Fiona whispered.

Julia and the other three stepped off the sidewalk and stood back. Darbie was still for a few seconds, and then she moved her feet, faster and faster, in little kicks and stomps while the rest of her body stayed straight and she kept her head faced forward.

"How cool is that?" Fiona said.

Maggie nodded. "I've seen that on TV."

"It must be Irish," Kitty said.

Sophie could almost feel her own Irish character—who so far had no name—holding her shamrock-dotted skirt up to her knees and moving her feet so fast the crowd could hardly see them. *When the music stopped, they all rushed to her—*

"You don't do it as good as Darbie does, Sophie," Maggie said.

"Come on," Fiona said as the bell rang. She linked her arm through Sophie's as they followed the crowd toward the door. "You were thinking Irish, weren't you?"

"We have to make an Irish film," Sophie said.

"Oh, definitely," Fiona said. "I'll find out stuff on the Internet."

Maggie looked over her shoulder at them as they shuffled their way into the hall. "We have to think of something for our showcase first."

"Shhh..." Kitty said. "Don't let the Pops hear we don't have our idea yet."

The Corn Pops were just ahead of them, but Sophie could see that they were way too focused on Darbie to give them a second thought.

"Can you teach us how to do that?" she heard Willoughby say to her.

"But we're not doing that for the showcase," Julia said—eyes flashing at Willoughby.

Anne-Stuart put her arm around Darbie's shoulder with a sniff. "We can teach you how to really dance. You're coordinated enough. It won't take that long."

Darbie stopped just inside the arts classroom and flung Anne-Stuart's arm away from her.

"I know how to 'really dance,' so I do," she said. "Would you ever lay off? Scram!"

Miss Blythe glided over to where the Flakes and Pops were now standing in two clumps with Darbie between them.

"Artistic differences?" Miss Blythe said. She made it sound like that was a good thing.

"Darbie's going to be in our group," Anne-Stuart said. "And we were just telling her—"

"—that I don't know how to dance."

"It's just not the right dance for us," Anne-Stuart said.

"—then cop on and find someone else," Darbie said.

The Corn Pops stared at her, probably because nobody ever said no to them. In the silence, Maggie spoke up.

"I'm doing costumes for you," she said to Julia.

Sophie could feel her eyes popping at Maggie. "You're doing costumes for them?"

"I don't WANT to," Maggie said, "but I HAVE to." She frowned. "It's my mom."

"Oh," Sophie said. She knew about parents and "have to's."

"My mom said if we didn't get an idea by today, I have to do costumes for the Po—for them."

"*What?*" Fiona said.

"That works out just perfectly then," Miss Blythe said. "Without Maggie, your group needs another person, Fiona. And since—what was your name, love?" She glanced at Darbie's NEW STUDENT slip.

Darbie's eyes turned to stones. "Darbie O'Grady," she said. "Not 'love.'"

Miss Blythe clasped her hands under her chin. Sophie wasn't sure what punctuation mark that was.

"Fabulous," Miss Blythe said. "Darbie O'Grady, you will work with Fiona and Kitty and Sophie. Maggie, you'll transfer to the Julia, B.J., Willoughby, and Anne-Stuart group."

When the Corn Flakes got to their table, Kitty was already whining like a cocker spaniel.

"Why did they have to steal Maggie? Who's going to make our costumes?"

"What costumes?" Fiona said. "We don't even have an idea yet."

"Now isn't that just brilliant." Darbie folded her arms across the front of her sweater. "I've gone from one set of eejits to another, so I have."

"I love how you talk," Kitty said to her. "Say something else."

Darbie didn't cooperate. She seemed to be chewing at the inside of her mouth.

"Do you miss being in Ireland?" Kitty said.

"That depends on whether she's from Ireland or Northern Ireland," Fiona said. She turned to Sophie. "They're two different countries."

"I told you Northern Ireland before," Darbie said, and then she clamped her teeth together.

"Oh—too bad," Fiona said.

"Why is it too bad?" Kitty said.

"It is not bad!" Darbie glared at each one of them in turn. "It's my home and I'll be thanking you not to be slagging it."

It wasn't hard to figure out what "slagging" meant. "We don't mean to," Sophie said. "We're just curious."

"Insatiably," Fiona said.

"It's because we love to make films about fascinating things," Sophie said. "Even though Miss Blythe won't let us do one for the showcase, we still want to make an Irish film for Corn Flakes Productions—that's what we're called."

"So you're only chatting me up so you can use me." Darbie's eyes were like flickers of heat lightning. "I wouldn't be part of one of your childish little pictures. You see ..." she lowered her voice so that the Corn Flakes had to tilt themselves toward her to hear. "I am not a child."

Four

It was a long-faced group that met at Fiona's house the next morning, Saturday, to try to make a decision about the showcase.

Fiona was annoyed because her little brother and sister, Rory and Isabella, were being even more heinous than usual, breaking in the new nanny, Ethel, who stood in the middle of the yard and yelled because she was the biggest human being in the world and couldn't run after them.

Kitty was all whimpery because Maggie wasn't there.

Sophie was still smoldering over the fact that the Corn Pops got to do what they were good at for the showcase, but the Corn Flakes couldn't.

And as for Darbie—it seemed to Sophie that she was sullen and annoyed and smoldering no matter what was going on.

It was a warm day for March. They were sprawled at the picnic table on Fiona's back deck with their juice boxes, sighing and staring, when Darbie gave her wristwatch a pointy look and said, "It's half eleven. We've sat here foostering about for an hour now."

Kitty giggled. "Half eleven? Does that mean eleven thirty?"

"It means we need to be getting on with it," Darbie said.

"You come up with something then," Fiona said.

Darbie shrugged. Fiona broke rule number one and rolled her eyes. Kitty giggled again, although as far as Sophie could see there was absolutely nothing funny. She could almost hear the poem Miss Blythe was going to assign them.

The door to the deck opened and Boppa, Fiona's grandfather, strolled toward them, a picnic basket in each hand. "How's the showcase coming along?" he said.

"It's not," Fiona said. "Let's face it—we're clueless."

"Sounds like you lasses need a break."

Boppa was wiggling his dark caterpillar eyebrows, but today not even Boppa and his comical faces could cheer up the Corn Flakes.

"Lasses?" Kitty said.

Boppa stopped next to Darbie and gave her his soft smile. "Do they still call young ladies 'lasses' in Ireland these days? It's been a while since I've been there. I don't want to be uncool."

"No," Darbie said between her teeth. "Not in NORTHERN Ireland."

"So you don't say 'wee' and 'bonnie' either?" Sophie said.

"Only American tourists who think they know everything talk that way in my country." Darbie's words came out tightly, as if she were constantly trying to swallow them back. "And I thought I told you I wasn't a specimen under a microscope."

"Doesn't anybody want to know where we're going to eat this lunch?" Boppa said.

"Uh, let me think," Fiona said. "Here at the table?"

"How does Gull Island sound?"

"Really?" Kitty said.

"That would be great, Boppa," Fiona said, "if we actually had a boat." She was just short of rolling her eyes. Fiona got a little cranky when she was frustrated.

"We do today. I rented a couple of rowboats so you could get out to the island for a picnic lunch."

Sophie jolted, knocking over her grape juice box. "A real boat? Does it have paddles?"

"It would be murder to row without them," Darbie said. She glared and set the box upright just before purple juice dripped out onto her sleeve.

But Sophie barely heard her. All through stuffing themselves into the black SUV—with Boppa, Ethel, Rory, and Izzy, and riding to Messick Point, Sophie could only think about Colleen O'Bravo, who was headed for adventure.

That's my Irish character's name, Sophie thought. *And Colleen isn't going to call people eejits, which I guess is a word for stupid people, but I'm sure not going to ask Darbie. Darbie's mean—Colleen isn't.*

While Boppa parked the car, Ethel led the group down a pier that stretched over the water, barking down at Izzy and Rory who she had clamped firmly by their forearms. She sounded like a jail warden, but Sophie tried to imagine her with an accent. *Maybe she was an Irish jail warden, and the Corn Flakes were trying to break Darbie out of prison, where she had been unjustly sent.* She wasn't sure how Rory and Izzy were going to fit in. Maybe they were rats ...

"I'll be in one boat with the two little ones," Ethel was shouting, "and Mr. Bunting will be in the other one with the rest of you." She sized Sophie up with her eyes. "You're little, so that boat can handle it."

"I'm not so sure the other one can handle HER," Fiona whispered to Sophie.

"Everybody put on a life jacket," Ethel shouted next.

Darbie opened her mouth just as Ethel shoved a blue puffy thing at her chest.

"I don't think you argue with her," Kitty whispered.

By the time Boppa joined them with the picnic baskets, the girls were all strapped into their jackets. Sophie's was so big even over her sweatshirt, she could barely see where she was going. Ethel was still trying to wrestle the two little ones into theirs.

"Any of you ever rowed a boat before?" Boppa said to the girls.

Darbie's hand shot up. Fiona raised hers too.

"When was that?" Boppa said to her.

"That one summer," Fiona said. "We went up to that lake place in Michigan. You weren't there."

"You get back here, Izzy, before you fall in and get soaked!"

Ethel thundered past them with Rory under one arm. Boppa pointed down to one of the boats.

"Get aboard," he said. "I'll be right back." Then he took off after Ethel, just in time to catch Rory kicking himself free.

"I'd throw both of those little blaggards into the drink," Darbie said as she led the way down the ladder.

"Don't you mean black guards?" Fiona said. "I think that's the way it's spelled."

Darbie shrugged. "Then maybe you shouldn't think."

Kitty gave one of her I'm-about-to-cry giggles. "Boppa said to get in the boat."

It took a few minutes to sort out the seating arrangements. Fiona said she should be in front so she could be captain, and Darbie should be at the other end to take orders. After Darbie was in her place at the back of the boat, she smirked and said Fiona could sit up in the bow if she wanted to, but if she expected to help row she had to sit there next to Darbie in the middle.

"I know," Fiona said. "I was just checking to be sure YOU knew."

"Right," Darbie said.

Sophie and Kitty sat in the stern—without oars—and Fiona told them to get on their knees and lean against the seat since that was the right way to do it.

"It would be if we were canoeing," Darbie said. "In this boat, you can sit on your bum."

"I have a 'bum'?" Kitty said.

"I think that's her word for bottom," Sophie said. She added that to her mental treasury of Colleen words.

Darbie nodded at the two oars which were attached to the boat through big metal clamps. Darbie called them *oarlocks.* "You're going to have to row precisely in time with me," she said to Fiona, "unless you fancy turning around in circles."

Sophie saw a smile escape from Darbie's dark eyes.

She's making fun of Fiona, Colleen O'Bravo thought. I will speak to her about that, I will, when we're alone. Then she settled on her bum and waited for the adventure to begin.

But that didn't promise to happen any time soon. Up on the dock, Ethel was holding Izzy between her knees as she tried to poke her arms through the life jacket holes. Boppa was working on Rory, and both kids were screaming, and Fiona's eyes were practically rolling right out of her head and into the water.

"She's got one done, so she does," Darbie said.

Boppa grabbed Izzy as she wriggled away from Ethel and held her by the back of the life jacket with one hand and Rory with the other. He was wrinkling his caterpillar eyebrows from Ethel to the boat and back again.

"He knows somebody's going to drown," Fiona said. "So much for this adventure."

"Could you drown here?" Kitty said. She pulled herself closer to Sophie. "How deep is it?"

"It's not but a meter or two deep right here," Darbie said.

"How do you know?" Fiona said.

"Because I live on the water. My kinfolk are fishermen," Darbie shot back.

"We don't talk in meters."

"Everybody else in the whole world does."

"Fiona."

Boppa was squatting on the dock, looking down at them.

"Ethel is going to stay here with Izzy, and I'm going to take Rory in the other boat. Can you follow me, do you think?"

"Absolutely," Fiona said. She grabbed up the oar. "Untie us, Sophie!"

"Cast off," Darbie said.

"WhatEVER," Fiona said back.

"I don't think they like each other that much," Kitty whispered to Sophie.

Sophie tried to imagine she was Colleen, unwrapping the rope from the barnacled deck and pushing against the piling with her hand to send them off, but it was impossible. Darbie and Fiona were definitely not in a dream world.

"You sure you know what you're doing?" Darbie said to Fiona.

"I told you, I've done it before," Fiona said.

Sophie watched Darbie push her oar backward over the water, dip it in, and pull it back.

"In time with me!" Darbie said.

"Why do you get to be the captain?" Fiona said.

"Go on, then."

Darbie pulled her oar out of the water. Fiona pushed hers down into the water and then lifted it up. The boat went backward.

"That's not the way Darbie did it," Kitty whispered to Sophie.

It didn't take a sailor to figure out Darbie's was the right way. The boat was now moving in a circle.

"You're making a bags of doing it!" Darbie called out. "Do it like this! Forward. Now in! Now back!"

"You got us going in circles!" Fiona shouted back.

"No—YOU do! Now quit blathering and do what I tell you!"

Fiona dragged her oar in the water, and the boat came to a stop. Kitty edged closer to Sophie.

"You all right back there?" Boppa was holding Rory between his feet and watching the girls.

"We're fine!" Fiona said.

Darbie gave a knot of a laugh. "We would be if you would admit you don't know what you're doing and listen to me!"

"Shut up!" Fiona said. "I know what I'm doing. This is an American boat—not Irish!"

"You're an eejit!"

Kitty clutched at Sophie's jeans and started to cry. At that point, Sophie had no choice. She had to escape into Colleen O'Bravo's world or she was going to push Darbie and Fiona and Kitty right into the shallows of the Chesapeake.

Why are they arguing about silly things when there's work to be done? Colleen thought. She didn't know exactly what work it was, what incredibly important mission she'd be assigned, but she certainly wasn't going to find out this way. Even though that angry Darbie O'Grady finally got the boat to move through the water in a straight line, her fellow crew members refused to con-

centrate on what their mission might be. Those two with the oars are too busy trying to both be captain, she thought with a little anger of her own. And I suppose it's up to me as always, to step in and settle things between them so we can get on with it. She gathered her shamrock-dotted skirts up around her knees and stood up, one foot on the bench where her bum had just been. "Now see here ..." she began. But they all screamed at her at once, even Kitty. In fact, she screamed loudest, as the boat lurched and—

—and Sophie tumbled backward into the water with Kitty still attached to her pant leg. All she could hear was Darbie yelling, "Are you gone in the head? Sit DOWN!"

Five

Sunday was a bumpy day, and it got rougher with each piece of news Sophie stumbled over.

Right after church, Kitty called, still wailing. As far as Sophie could tell, she hadn't stopped bawling since before the boat had even dumped them out.

"No offense, Kitty," Sophie said, "but are you still crying? You hardly even went under the water. You were wearing a life jacket!"

"That's not what's wrong!" Kitty said. She sounded like a cat being bathed in the sink.

Sophie sighed. "Then what is wrong?"

"My dad said I can't go over to Fiona's anymore!"

"*What?* Why?"

"Because her parents didn't watch us."

"Her parents never watch us. They're not even there most of the time."

"Yeah. That's what my dad said. He said I could've drowned, and he's not taking any more chances."

Sophie nibbled at her lip. This wasn't the time to point out that if Kitty hadn't carried on so much when her dad had arrived to pick her up, he probably wouldn't have thought she'd been near death.

"Are you guys going to stop being my friend because I can't go to Fiona's?" Kitty said, winding up again.

"Hello! You're a Corn Flake!" Sophie said.

That seemed to calm Kitty down for the time being.

The next phone call was from Fiona. She wasn't crying, as far as Sophie could tell.

"My mom and dad fired Ethel," she said, voice cheery. "It's because she can't control the brats." Fiona gave a soft snort. "I could've told them that."

"That means another new nanny," Sophie said. "I wish Kateesha hadn't quit. I liked her."

"So did her fiancé. They went off and got married, which I think is dumb. Anyway, here's the bad news: Boppa has to watch the two little morons until my parents get around to hiring somebody, so no more Boppa adventures for us for a while. We can't even meet out at my house."

Sophie sagged against the step she was sitting on with the phone. "It's all my fault."

"They didn't terminate her because of the boat thing," Fiona said. "That stuff happens, they said. Besides, you're not to blame — Darbie is. She just thinks she's the boss of us, that's all, and she didn't even know what she was doing."

"I'm the one who freaked out and stood up!" Sophie said. *Gone in the head*, was the way Darbie had said it.

Fiona's voice went down to secret level. "And I know why too. You were coming up with a new character—somebody Irish, right? What's her name?"

Before Sophie could answer, she heard what sounded like the Tasmanian Devil on Fiona's end of the line.

"I have to go help Boppa shut them up," Fiona said. "Mom was up all night doing surgery on somebody's stomach. She is not going to be happy if they wake her up."

Sophie turned off the phone and curled up miserably on the step. All she wanted to do was slip into Colleen's world, where she wasn't responsible for nannies getting fired and people's dads saying they couldn't go to other people's houses. But as deliciously as Colleen beckoned to her with her red ringlets dancing—she had to have her hair in red ringlets—Sophie felt an old uneasy squirminess in her stomach. Colleen might be brave and determined and ready to take any risk for the cause—whatever that might be—but she could also get Sophie into a lot of trouble, and Sophie knew it. First would be the escapes into Colleen's world—then the bad grades—then the loss of the camera.

And she and the Corn Flakes would still end up reciting "Mary Had a Little Lamb" for the stupid showcase.

There's only one person who can help me now, she decided as she uncurled herself from the step. *I need to tell Mama and Daddy it's time for me to go back to Dr. Peter.*

The only two good things about the day so far were that Lacie was still away on her youth group retreat and Zeke was taking a nap. Those were God signs, as far as Sophie was concerned. She never, ever had Mama and Daddy all to herself.

She found them both in the family room, faces in the Sunday paper. When Sophie slipped onto the couch beside Mama, she folded the paper in her lap. Daddy woke up behind his.

"I need to talk to you," Sophie said. "Dr. Peter said I could come see him any time I started back into my old habits, and I've started."

She drew in a huge breath. Daddy tossed the paper to the floor and leaned forward in the big chair with his hands folded between his blue-jeaned knees.

"Good job, coming to us before it got out of hand, Soph," he said. "That's heads-up ball." Daddy always talked like the whole family was playing in the Super Bowl.

"Then Mama can make me an appointment?" Sophie said. "For tomorrow?"

Her parents did that thing they always did—looking at each other over the top of her head like they were having an entire conversation without saying a word. Kind of the way she and Fiona did sometimes.

"You know, Dream Girl," Mama said, "Daddy and I have been seeing Dr. Peter too, and we can probably help you with this."

Sophie nodded slowly. Dr. Peter had mentioned that, come to think of it. Still—she pulled a strand of hair under her nose.

"What?" Daddy said. "Come on, give us the goods."

"I don't know if you can do it like Dr. Peter," Sophie said.

Daddy grinned at Mama. "You have to admit, she's honest."

"You haven't seen us in action," Mama said. "We've been waiting for an opportunity like this."

"We've been in training." Daddy flexed his arm muscles, and a giggle slipped out of Sophie.

"What?" Daddy said. "What's funny?"

"So—you'll really, like, help me and not just take the camera away if my grades drop?"

"Absolutely," Mama said.

"All right, let's go—bring it on," Daddy said.

Mama got out some lemon bars and milk, and Sophie launched into the story. By the time she got to the part about Fiona's parents firing Ethel, she was feeling like she *was* talking to Dr. Peter. Mama and Daddy were listening and nodding, and they didn't interrupt once.

And then the front door burst open, slapping against the wall—and Lacie appeared.

She wasn't alone. There was a lady behind her with a face so twisted in anger, it took Sophie a minute to realize it was Lacie's best friend Valerie's mom. An *uh-oh* took shape in

Sophie's mind. Mrs. Bonningham had been a chaperone on the youth group retreat.

Mama and Daddy must have seen the smoke coming out of the lady's ears too, because they skipped the whole how-was-the-trip-what-are-you-doing-home-so-early thing and went straight to "What's wrong?"

Lacie opened her mouth, but it was Mrs. Bonningham who spewed out several paragraphs worth of stuff about Lacie being caught outside her cabin, after curfew, with a BOY.

"We weren't doing anything!" Lacie managed to get in. "We were just talking!" Even her freckles were pale.

"What were you thinking?" Daddy said. His face was watermelon red.

"Whatever it was, they were all thinking the same thing," Mrs. Bonningham said. "Half the kids were off someplace, and most of them weren't 'just talking.' "

Sophie didn't even want to *think* about what that meant.

Mrs. Bonningham pulled her neck up in a stiff way. "Let's just say the whole thing was less than spiritually focused. I don't think I heard God mentioned a single time except when they were blessing the food."

"It was just supposed to be fun!" Lacie wailed.

"Well, the fun's about to be over," Daddy said.

He ushered Lacie up the stairs, and Mama steered Mrs. Bonningham toward the front door. When Mama too had hurried up the steps to Lacie's room, Sophie was left on the couch with a half-empty plate of lemon bars. They were the last thing she wanted.

Here we go again, she thought as she trudged up to her own room. *Lacie has a crisis and instantly it's all about her. Forget about the devastation that's happening in MY life!*

Although she was way tempted to jump with both feet into Colleen's world and forget about her own currently miserable one, Sophie flopped down on her bed and tried to think what Dr. Peter would tell her to do.

Du-uh, she thought, hitting herself on the forehead with the heel of her hand. *He'd say, "Have you read that Bible story, Loodle?"*

She pulled out her Bible and turned each thin page between the tips of her fingers. She always did that. It seemed more sacred that way.

"Okay, John thirteen," she said out loud — mostly to drown out the deep thunder of Daddy's voice rolling out of Lacie's room next door. She didn't see how Zeke was sleeping through all this.

The pages splashed softly to chapter 13, verse 1, and Sophie read.

It was just before the Passover Feast. Jesus knew that the time had come for him to leave this world and go to the Father. Having loved his own who were in the world, he now showed them the full extent of his love.

Sophie stopped and closed her eyes. Dr. Peter had taught her to pretend she was somebody in the story, which was challenging this time, seeing how all the disciples were boys. Trying not to think about the Fruit Loops, Sophie changed her name to Luke and pulled her hair under her nose like a mustache. It wasn't her favorite role, but at least she got to be with Jesus. She read on.

The evening meal was being served ... Jesus got up from the meal, took off his outer clothing —

Yikes! Sophie thought. *Okay, that has to be just like a jacket or something.*

Sophie got a firmer grip on the sides of the Bible and focused hard on being Luke.

Sophie/Luke read on, scratching at his mustache.

Jesus wrapped a towel around his waist. After that, he poured water into a basin and began to wash his disciples' feet, drying them with the towel that was wrapped around him.

Sophie/Luke yanked his feet back as Jesus worked his way down the table toward him. *My feet are way dirty!* he thought. *I've been running around in sandals all day! This is SO embarrassing!*

And then suddenly, Jesus was right there next to him, reaching out for Simon Peter's ankle. Simon Peter said to him,

"Lord, are you going to wash my feet?"

That's what I wanna know! Sophie/Luke thought. He pulled the edges of his dirty robe over the tips of his toes.

Jesus replied, "You do not realize now what I am doing, but later you will understand."

I sure hope so, thought Sophie/Luke. Right now his mind felt like a bowl of pudding.

"No," said Peter, "you shall never wash my feet."

Tell him, Peter! Sophie/Luke wanted to cry out. Tell him we're not worthy to have our Master touch our filthy feet! After all, if anyone could change Jesus' mind, it was Peter. He was the biggest and the strongest.

Jesus answered, "Unless I wash you, you have no part with me."

"Then, Lord," Simon Peter replied, "Not just my feet but my hands and my head as well!"

Let me just jump right into the bowl! Sophie/Luke thought. *That's how much help I need right now!*

Sophie stopped and scanned down the page with her finger. When was she going to get to the part where the answer to the showcase problem was?

She stopped at verse 12. *When he had finished washing their feet he put on his clothes and returned to his place.* Sophie/Luke watched his every move. The answer was sure to come right from the Master's lips.

"Now that I, your Lord and Teacher, have washed your feet, you also should wash one another's feet. I have set you an example that you should do as I have done for you."

Sophie blinked and let her "mustache" drop to her shoulder. That was all Dr. Peter had said to read. But what did any of that have to do with the major catastrophe she was in the middle of?

She tried to picture herself taking a bowl and pitcher to school tomorrow and breaking it out in arts class and washing Kitty's and Fiona's and Darbie's feet. Miss Blythe might think it was artistic genius, but the Corn Pops—not to mention Darbie—would roll their eyes right up into their brains.

I would so do it, Jesus, Sophie thought. *I totally would. Only, I just don't get how it's going to help us come up with an idea and keep me out of trouble.*

There was a shriek from next door, which popped the image of Jesus out of Sophie's head like a pin in a bubble. It was Lacie, begging for mercy.

"PLEASE don't make me drop softball!" she was practically screaming. "I have to play—I have to—Coach was gonna pick me as team captain."

Mama's voice murmured something and Daddy's muttered something back and Lacie went into a new burst of hysterical tears. Sophie figured there must be a flood in that room by now.

This could go on forever, Sophie thought as she threw herself back against her pillows. *So much for Mama and Daddy helping me with my problem.*

She closed her eyes and let Colleen in, tossing her red ringlets and assuring Sophie that everything would turn out, it just would.

But as Sophie donned her green top hat, she thought again of Dr. Peter.

She needed him, and she needed him now.

Six

The next three days were so foot-stomping frustrating, Sophie wanted to pitch a fit about every other minute. But Lacie was doing enough of that for both of them.

Whenever Mama and Daddy weren't both dealing *with* Lacie, they were talking to each other *about* Lacie. Or they were on the phone discussing with other people the whole church youth group "situation."

What about MY situation? Sophie wanted to scream more than once.

One of those times was Monday, when right in front of everybody before school on the playground, the Pops acted out the whole arm scene they had witnessed the Flakes doing on the stage that one morning. They didn't use names, but everybody knew, because there wasn't a kid gathered there who didn't turn and gape at the Corn Flakes or laugh so hard they were spewing spit, like the Fruit Loops did.

"Those boys could be a little more obnoxious," Fiona muttered to Sophie, "but I don't know how."

And then, during arts class, while the Corn Flakes continued to scribble down ideas and crumple them up and feel lamer by the minute, the Pops got to go to the stage and practice their dance.

"Like they really need to practice," Maggie told the Corn Flakes after class. "I watched them rehearse all weekend—and you want to know what?"

"No," Fiona said. "But tell us anyway."

Maggie pulled her head forward, and so did Sophie, Kitty, and Fiona. "Their parents are spending so much money on fabric for the costumes," she whispered. "I'm not supposed to tell you what they're going to look like, but they're expensive."

Right on cue, Kitty whimpered.

By Tuesday, the Corn Flake group still hadn't come up with an idea, and Darbie had grown more and more "disdain-ful," as Fiona put it.

"Does that mean she thinks we're absurd and stupid and lame?" Sophie said before school.

"Pretty much."

"I don't like her," Kitty whispered—even though they were huddled in a far corner of the school yard and Darbie wasn't even outside. "I don't like her at all."

"Yeah, but we're stuck with her," Fiona said. She wig-gled her eyebrows. "As soon as the showcase is over though, whammo—she's out of here. We don't ever even have to talk to her again."

Sophie toyed with the string on her hooded sweatshirt.

"What, Soph?" Fiona said. "Don't tell me you want to be friends with her! She acts like we have head lice or something. She's as bad as the Corn Pops."

"Only she treats them the same way she does us," Sophie said.

"I even saw her blow Harley and them off," Kitty said. "She just doesn't like anybody."

"I don't get it," Sophie said.

Fiona pulled a splinter of wood off the fence and poked it at the ground. "We don't have to 'get it.' If she doesn't want to be friends with anybody, then what are we supposed to do?"

Wash her feet, Sophie thought.

She put her hand over her mouth, just in case she had said it out loud, but neither Kitty nor Fiona was looking at her like she suddenly had three nostrils, so she figured she was safe. That thought had been pretty crazy, even for her.

But it wouldn't leave her alone all day Tuesday: *Everybody needs at least one friend*. When she herself had moved to Poquoson from Houston, all she'd wanted was one girlfriend who would understand her and not think she was whacked out—and she had prayed for that even before Dr. Peter had taught her about talking to Jesus. Then, just like in one of her own daydreams, Fiona had suddenly been there.

Sophie wasn't sure what to do with that. But during social studies, when Ms. Quelling assigned a country project, she decided it couldn't hurt to pick Ireland. She was the first one in line for the library.

She found one book that had information about Northern Ireland too, and she burrowed into it before the bell rang. She found out that Irish people dug up some kind of dirt called peat to use for firewood, and that the whole country had almost died out when there had been a potato famine back in 1845. That tickled up a scene for the film, but it didn't help much when she got to arts class and Darbie demanded to know just HOW they were going to make a holy show of themselves in the showcase.

"I know we will," she said, arms folded across her sweater. "It's only a matter of how we're to be mortified."

Sophie didn't want to wash Darbie's feet at that point. It was one of those moments when she had the urge to clench her fists and stomp her foot and scream, "Then why don't you think of something if you're so smart!"

She didn't have to. Fiona did it. Darbie told her she didn't need to eat the head off her. Then Kitty started crying. And Miss Blythe floated over to them and assured them that the best art was born out of frustration.

Miss Blythe walked toward the Fruit Loops, calling, "Art is discipline, boys!"

Darbie scowled. "I don't want to give birth to art, thank you very much."

She said "much" like "mooch." Sophie made a note to talk like that when she was being Colleen O'Bravo. At the moment, Colleen had "mooch" to be concerned about.

Would there be enough peat for the winter? Would there be a peat shortage, just as there had been a five-year potato famine those many years ago that had almost brought Ireland to ruin? Some of her own ancestors had come to America because of that—and now she was here too—and no one seemed to understand her a bit—

"You—Sophie!"

Sophie tossed Colleen's red ringlets out of her face and stared blankly at Darbie.

"I thought you'd gone into a bit of a trance," Darbie said. "I hope you were coming up with something."

"She will," Kitty said. "She always does."

All Darbie did was grunt.

At home that night, it was impossible for Sophie to think about the showcase, much less come up with something. Lacie and Mama and Daddy were having yet another "discussion" in Lacie's room, and Sophie had to watch Zeke in her room and try to do her homework at the same time. At least she got to read about Northern Ireland, although Zeke made even that pretty hard when he tried to climb up Sophie's curtains like

Spider-Man. Finally, she made him sit next to her on the floor and listen while she read the book out loud.

"'The splitting of Ireland into the Republic of Ireland and Northern Ireland took place in 1921,'" she read.

"Was I born yet?" Zeke said.

"No. Mama and Daddy weren't even born yet. I don't know anybody that was born then." Sophie patted the top of Zeke's head. "You have to listen. We're about to get to the good part."

"Is Spider-Man in it?"

"No!"

Zeke's dark eyebrows came down into upside-down Vs. "Then how's it going to get good?"

Sophie ran her eyes down the page. "Because they started fighting," she said. "About absolutely EVERYTHING — for Pete's sake — whether they were Protestant or Catholic — who liked England and who didn't — I don't even GET most of this stuff."

"Who are the bad guys?"

"Who can tell?" Sophie studied the page.

"There have to be bad guys if there's fighting. How do the good guys win if there's no bad guys?"

"I'm getting to that."

"Well, hurry up!" Zeke got up on his knees beside her and thumped the page with his chubby index finger.

"Okay, okay! Let's see — people live separate from people who don't believe like they do — like, behind cement walls and iron gates and stuff. People throw bombs over the walls — "

Sophie stopped and sucked in a breath. Did Darbie live like that? With burned-out houses all around her, like the book said?

"Spider-Man will save 'em from bombs!" Zeke cried.

"Don't start climbing the walls yet. There's more." Sophie repositioned her glasses. She felt herself frowning and ignored

Zeke's new ascent up the side of the mattress. "It got REALLY ugly way back in 1969—I don't even know if Mama and Daddy were born by then. People were killing each other, Zeke. The British Army had to come up there and try to stop it."

Zeke stopped in mid-crawl across the bedspread. "You mean, like soldiers?"

"Yeah, right in front of their houses and stuff. They're still there!"

"Not after Spider-Man gets there!"

Zeke took a leap toward the dresser, but Sophie's mind was latched onto the image of Darbie, running past soldiers when she went to catch the bus for school. It made Sophie shiver.

The door opened just after Zeke hit the floor with a five-year-old thud.

"Hey, buddy, try to save the pieces, would you?" Daddy said. "So I can repair the floor after you fall through it." He looked at Sophie. "We're almost done—don't let Spider-Man get too carried away, okay?"

Colleen O'Bravo nodded, but her mind was far from the exploits of a small boy living out his daydreams. She had important things to attend to—like how to wash the feet of an Irish girl who had grown up with soldiers marching down her street, and trying to keep people from making bombs and throwing them into each other's neighborhoods.

After all, the great Irish doctor had given her the secret coded message. She had to treat her the way the Master, Jesus, had treated his friends.

When she woke up the next morning, Sophie knew exactly how she was going to do that. When she asked her mother, Mama's eyes got all soft the way they did every Mother's Day when the three kids lined up with their made-in-school presents.

"I'll have everything ready," she said. She hugged the Ireland book Sophie handed to her. "Thanks for the information."

At school, Sophie told the Corn Flakes and Darbie that they had to meet at her house after school and come to a final decision, before Miss Blythe slapped "Twinkle, Twinkle, Little Star" on them Thursday. Fiona cornered Sophie at their lockers in the back of Mr. Denton's room and whispered, "You can't keep stuff from your best friend. I know you too well. What's really going to happen at your house?"

Sophie pulled some hair under her nose.

"Now I know something's going on!" Fiona's eyes drooped. "How come you're keeping this a secret from me?"

"I just want it to be a surprise," Sophie said. *Besides*, she added to herself, *you might try to talk me out of it.*

And when she saw Fiona slit her eyes toward Darbie as she slid into her seat in the classroom, Sophie knew she was right. This had to happen for more than just one reason.

The day dragged on like it was hauling three backpacks' worth of homework behind it — but finally they were all piling into the LaCroix's Suburban after sixth period and Mama was making sure everybody had called home for permission.

"I talked to your mom personally," Mama said to Darbie.

"She's not my ma," Darbie said between her teeth.

"Who is she?" Kitty said.

"Can you ever lay off?" Darbie said.

Sophie decided that qualified as eating the head off Kitty.

"How was everyone's day?" Mama sang out.

"Getting worse by the minute," Fiona whispered to Sophie. "This better be good."

It looked like it was going to be. The instant the group got to Sophie's family room, Sophie knew Mama had read the Ireland book cover to cover. There was a green tablecloth on the big square coffee table along with a white teapot with shamrocks on it, and a stack of tea bags all labeled Irish

Breakfast Tea. Beside a plate of cloud-shaped biscuits was a vase full of tinted-green carnations and clover. Mama even had music playing that made Sophie want to dance the way they'd seen Darbie do for the Corn Pops.

"Welcome, Darbie," Mama said. "Sophie wanted to give you an Irish-American party. This might not be exactly the way it was in your home, but—"

"I love this!" Kitty said, with a Kitty-squeal. "Can I pour the tea?"

"Okay—I have to admit—this is pretty cool," Fiona said. Her eyes lit up like birthday-candle flames. "Let's all pick Irish names! I bet Sophie already has hers."

"Colleen O'Bravo," Sophie said. She smiled at Darbie. "Does that sound Irish?"

"No," Darbie said. "It sounds like some little-girlish thing you fancied out of the air." She looked at the tea things Mama had set up. "This isn't anything like Northern Ireland."

"Hello! Rude!" Fiona said.

But before Fiona could finish the step she started to take toward Darbie, Sophie was wedged between them, so close to Darbie she could see her nose hairs.

"It *is* little-girlish, Darbie!" Sophie said. "Because we are little girls—and all we're trying to do is make you feel like you have friends because that's what we do."

"Well, perhaps you are little girls," Darbie said. "But I am not. I never had a chance to be a little girl—and I don't even know HOW!"

Her eyes flashed down at Sophie just long enough for Sophie to see tears. And then Darbie turned and ran, slamming the front door behind her.

Seven

Mama sorted things out as only Mama could do. Within five minutes, Kitty's mom was picking her and Fiona up and taking them home, and Mama was on her way out to the Suburban with Darbie, who was shaking like a puppy.

"I just want to go home is all," she kept saying. "Please — let me go home."

It was way too hard to stay in the family room with the untouched Irish Breakfast Tea. Sophie flung herself facedown across her bed and was just starting to get Colleen O'Bravo into focus when Lacie threw herself down beside Sophie.

"How do you stand it when you get grounded?" she moaned.

Sophie frowned into the purple bedspread. "I just do."

"They aren't making me quit softball, but they grounded me for ten days! I'm already bored out of my skull!"

"It's not that bad," Sophie said. She brought her head up and rested it on her hand. "It gives me more time to come up with ideas for movies."

Lacie lifted her face, and Sophie expected an eye roll, but instead Lacie peered closely at her. "You know something?" she said. "Since you started making those films all the time, you hardly ever get grounded anymore. Weird."

"Yeah," Sophie said. "But I can't do a film right now, and I'm scared I'm going to get in trouble again."

"You don't even know what trouble is," Lacie said. She propped herself up on her elbows. "Not only did I get grounded for what happened at the retreat, but it'll probably get our youth leader in trouble too. Daddy's going to a meeting at church about it tonight. He says we might change churches if they don't start being more about God—but I love that church! That's where all my friends are!" She turned stormy eyes on Sophie. "I liked it better when you were the one getting in trouble all the time."

At least you're getting Mama and Daddy to yourself, Sophie thought. *I'm the one who needs them right now—not you!*

Lacie rolled onto her back and watched Sophie for a minute.

"I'm sorry," she said suddenly. "I didn't mean to make it sound like you were a total loser. I'm the loser at this point—I HATE this!"

She hauled herself off the bed and threw herself out of Sophie's room and into her own. Sophie could hear her crying through the wall.

It was the first time Sophie had ever thought she knew just how Lacie felt.

But I haven't time to go to her, Colleen O'Bravo thought. I have Darbie to think about now—and she's hurting worse than Lacie, she is. And there's the problem of the project too. I'm thinking it's time we went to the Master.

But Sophie had only just gotten Jesus' kind eyes into view when she heard the front door open. Mama was talking to someone, and it obviously wasn't Zeke. Her voice, trailing up the stairwell, was low and sad.

"Sophie?" she said. "Come on down—we have company."

By the time Sophie got downstairs, Mama was already in the family room — with Darbie and a lady who had her arm around Darbie so tightly she had to be her "ma."

"Shall I warm up the tea?" Mama said.

The lady looked at Darbie, who was staring at the floor and shaking her head. The second Sophie set her foot on the family room carpet, Darbie let go with a flood of tears that made no sound.

"Did I do something to hurt her feelings?" Sophie said to Darbie's ma.

"No, honey," the lady said. She didn't talk like Darbie at all. She sounded like someone who had been born and raised right there in Poquoson. She looked that way too, with her blonde hair flipped up everywhere and her frosty lipstick put on so perfectly it didn't go outside the lines of her lips.

Sophie looked at Mama for some magic words. Mama patted the sofa beside her and hugged Sophie's arm when she sat down.

"Darbie's pretty upset, but it isn't at you," Mama said. "Mrs. O'Grady is going to explain why."

"You can call me Aunt Emily," the lady said. She pronounced "aunt" like "ont." "That's what Darbie calls me."

Sophie had at least twenty-five questions raising their hands in her head, but she just nodded. She was afraid any word from her would start Darbie shaking again.

"I don't know how much you know about the Troubles in Northern Ireland," Aunt Emily said.

Sophie told her what she'd learned from the book, and Aunt Emily gave Mama a wide-eyed look. Even Darbie glanced up before she lowered her wet eyelashes toward the floor again.

"Sophie wanted to know everything she could about Darbie," Mama said.

"Then you'll understand Darbie's story, Sophie," Aunt Emily said. "Darbie's father—that would be my husband's brother—was very involved in trying to stop the fighting in Belfast in the 1980s. He was killed right after Darbie was born, just before the cease-fire was declared." She ran a manicured hand up and down Darbie's back. "He would have been so happy to see a move toward the peace he worked so hard for. There is still violence, but it was progress, and it had his fingerprints on it."

I bet Darbie doesn't even remember her dad, Sophie thought. As much as Daddy drove her nuts sometimes, she couldn't imagine never even knowing him.

"Darbie's mother carried on his work," Aunt Emily went on. "She helped start the Women's Coalition, which was very important in reaching the Belfast Agreement of 1998." Aunt Emily squeezed Darbie against her. "She was quite a lady, your mother, wasn't she?"

For the first time, Darbie lifted her face. Darbie was so close to Aunt Emily, Sophie was sure she probably went cross-eyed as she looked at her, but it seemed to stop her lips from trembling. She didn't move as Aunt Emily almost whispered the rest.

"And then, just six months ago, Darbie's mother died in a car accident. After growing up poor and without a father in the midst of so much violence, I think that was the hardest thing of all." She pulled Darbie's face into her chest and looked over her head at Sophie and Mama. "Harder than anything a little girl should have to go through."

Mama slipped her hand into Sophie's, and Sophie could feel her crying right down to her fingertips.

"My husband and I went to Northern Ireland and brought Darbie back here to live with us," Aunt Emily said. "I've been homeschooling her, and now that she has her bearings a little bit we thought it would be good for her to be in public school so she can make some friends."

Darbie turned her head and glanced at Sophie. Her eyes looked ashamed.

"She told me you have tried to include her," Aunt Emily said, "but it's so hard for her to trust people."

"Well, not only that," Mama said. "For heaven's sake, she hasn't lived the life the girls here have lived. No wonder she thought their group was 'little-girlish.'"

Aunt Emily nodded and went on into something Sophie didn't hear. Sophie could see so clearly in her mind Darbie locking all the doors and windows twenty times to keep out the people who hated her mother—and boiling the water for corned beef and cabbage while she waited for her ma to come home from her Coalition meeting, afraid to go out because she might be hit with a brick.

And praying that she wasn't riddled with bullets, the way her father was. If her mother was killed too, she wouldn't have anybody. Nobody to protect her from bombs and broken bottles being thrown. She could hear Darbie praying, "Jesus, please don't let them take my ma too—"

"Honey, are you all right?"

Sophie looked up at Aunt Emily through a blur of tears.

"I didn't mean to make you cry. I just wanted you to understand—"

"I do!" Sophie said. "And I hate it for her! I hate it for you, Darbie."

And then there was nothing else to say.

Not until Darbie slowly lifted herself out of her aunt's arms and shoved the tears from her cheeks with stiff fingers.

"I hate to cry," Darbie said. "I never cry." She whipped her face to meet Aunt Emily's. "But you were right—it feels good!"

After that, Darbie sobbed and sobbed, so hard that Mama and Sophie went into the kitchen to warm up the tea so she and Aunt Emily could be alone.

Mama stroked Sophie's cheek. "She says this is the first time she's seen Darbie cry since her mama died. This is a good thing."

"Is it okay if I tell Fiona and Kitty and Maggie?" Sophie said.

"I think you should ask Darbie," Mama said.

"I hope she says yes—because then they'd understand why she doesn't want to be friends with anybody here—why she ... like ... doesn't trust anybody." She gnawed at her lower lip. "Especially Fiona."

Mama poured hot water from the microwave into the teapot and looked at Sophie through the steam. "You know what, Soph? I think you've figured out what Darbie's parents were trying to do. They just wanted people to understand so they would stop fighting." She set down the water and folded her arms on the counter to look into Sophie's eyes. "Have you decided on anything for the showcase yet?"

Sophie shook her head. She'd forgotten all about that.

"What about helping all the kids understand about Darbie—if she approves it. Y'all are so good at acting things out."

"You would ask Miss Blythe to let us do a movie?" Sophie said.

Mama smiled her wispy smile and picked up the tea tray. "Who says you have to act it out on film?" she said.

Sophie trailed behind her to the family room, wailing out questions.

"But we never did it live before! What if we mess up? What if Kitty forgets her lines? She always forgets her lines!"

Mama turned to her just as they got to the door. "For heaven's sake, Dream Girl—use your imagination."

Darbie had stopped crying when they went in, and she was blowing her nose on a shamrock-covered paper napkin. She stuffed it into her pocket when she saw Sophie. "Do you think I'm completely gone in the head?" Darbie said.

"How about no!" Sophie said. "I think you're amazing—and not just like you're a specimen under a microscope."

"Excuse me?" Aunt Emily said.

"So if you hate this idea for our showcase, just tell me," Sophie said. "I can take it."

"Carry on, then," Darbie said.

Sophie glanced at Mama, got the nod, and told Darbie about the idea.

"It wouldn't be like using you," she said when she was almost out of breath. "It would be so other kids could understand."

Darbie leaned forward, her now-puffy eyes drilling into Sophie. "Would it get those ridiculous popettes to stop acting the maggot with me?" she said.

"The Corn Pops?" Sophie could feel a smile forming, because she was pretty sure what "acting the maggot" meant. "It might," she said.

"Then I say we stop foostering about and do it," Darbie said.

She stuck out her hand, and Sophie shook it. Darbie's fingers were hard and firm, like a grown-up's. It made Sophie feel sad for the little girl she never got to be.

Eight

Sophie and Darbie vowed to present their idea to the Corn Flakes the next morning before school. Sophie insisted they include Maggie so she wouldn't feel left out.

"We Corn Flakes take care of each other's feelings," Sophie told Darbie.

"Fair play!" Darbie said.

Sophie had a feeling that meant she was impressed.

The next day was March-rainy, so they met backstage—and early, in case the Corn Pops decided to come in and rehearse.

"They think they own the stage now," Kitty said when they were situated on the hay bales. "Hurry up, Sophie—tell us the idea before they come."

"I don't know why you couldn't have just told us over the phone," Fiona said. She pulled a Pop-Tart from her backpack and took a huge hunk out of it with her teeth.

No wonder she's grumpy this morning, Sophie thought. *She hasn't had breakfast.* It was obvious there was no new nanny yet.

While Fiona chewed sullenly, Sophie and Darbie unfolded the story of Darbie's life in Northern Ireland and what they wanted to do with it onstage.

"My dad said he would film it for us so we could still have a movie," Sophie said. "This is gonna be our *real*est one yet."

She wisped a smile over at Darbie, who gave her one back.

"We'll get it right down to the wee details," Darbie said.

"Wow."

They all turned to look at Maggie.

"I wish I was still in this group," she said.

For the first time that morning, Sophie saw Fiona's face light up. "Does the Corn Pops' dance stink?"

"No. It's way good. But *I* don't have anything to do with it. I'm making the costumes by myself. Me and my mom. And all the Corn Pops do is fight all the time." She shrugged. "Every one of them says they want to beat you guys for first prize—so you would think they would agree since they all want the same thing. But then they start yelling, and somebody is always crying." She looked at Kitty. "Willoughby cries more than you do."

"All right then," Fiona said, chin firm. "One thing we have going for us is unity. We can so beat them."

Sophie cut her eyes sideways at Darbie, who was studying Fiona like she was a textbook.

"Right," Sophie said slowly. "We'll make everybody understand about how it's stupid to fight over being different." She inserted a nod. "That's our mission."

"And we have only eight days to do it," Fiona said, though Sophie had the feeling Fiona hadn't even heard her. "We have to practice every day after school and the whole weekend."

"But not at your house," Kitty said. "Remember my dad."

"It wouldn't work anyway," Fiona said. "Not without a nanny for the brats. Okay, so who doesn't have annoying siblings running around to drive us nuts?"

"I don't," Darbie said. "You can come to my house."

Fiona tapped her bow of a mouth with her fingertip. "Where do you live?"

"What does that matter?" Darbie said.

For a moment, Fiona's eyes narrowed and nearly met at the bridge of her nose. Just as Sophie began to wriggle on top of her hay bale, Fiona shook her head. "I guess we don't have any other choice."

Sophie felt as if a shadow had just passed over the stage, although it lifted some when they found Miss Blythe in the hall and told her their plan. She pressed her jangling hand to her collarbone, closed her eyes, and said, "Brilliant. Absolutely brilliant." Then she told them they had to have a script for her by Monday.

"That is absolutely no problem," Fiona assured her. "Sophie and I have had a plethora of experience writing scripts."

."What's a 'plethora'?" Darbie said when Miss Blythe had sailed off.

"It means more than anybody else," Fiona said. She didn't have to say *including you*. Sophie could see it glinting in her gray eyes.

They started work at Darbie's house that very afternoon. After all, it was only four days until the script was due.

Darbie's aunt and uncle's place was right on the Poquoson River, a rambling, two-story house made of white boards that looked as if they'd just been painted. There were four boats of different sizes moored at the dock in the backyard.

"We aren't going to put a boat scene in this, are we?" Kitty asked, gazing nervously out the back window as she sipped the limeade that pretty, perky Aunt Emily had fixed for them — green to put them in an Irish mood, with real lime slices hooked on the sides of the glasses.

"We couldn't do that on a stage, Kitty," Sophie told her gently — before Fiona could get an eye roll in. She currently seemed to be looking for a chance to roll them around at somebody.

Darbie led them to a paneled room that was lined with books and had a telescope in the window—since, as she put it, her bedroom was in a "desperate condition." Sophie made a note to herself to include as many of Darbie's expressions as possible in the script. *I've already learned most of Fiona's words,* she thought. *Now I have all this new vocabulary.*

Fiona opened the Treasure Book and whipped out a pen. "Since Maggie isn't here, I'll write everything down. I think we should start the film—oops, play—where Darbie's a baby—"

"A little thing," Sophie put in.

"—and her father gets killed. Darbie could play her own mom and be holding a baby doll. Izzy has like a hundred of them—"

"But how will they know why my father was killed?" Darbie said.

"You mean background," Fiona said. She wafted the pen in the air with a flourish. "We'll just put that in the program for people to read. It would be too boring to tell it."

"Not the way Sophie does it," Darbie said.

Sophie was beginning to like the way Darbie pronounced her name—Soophie. She decided to ask Fiona and Kitty later to say it that way from now on.

"Tell them the way you told it to my aunt yesterday," Darbie said to Sophie.

"That's not how you do a play though," Fiona said. She tapped her chin with the end of the gel pen as if she were waiting for Darbie to get that so they could move on.

Sophie cocked her head at Fiona. "But somebody could be telling that at the front of the stage while Darbie's father was walking along, and then other people could come out and jump him—you know, like, what's that called?"

"You mean pantomime?" One side of Fiona's lip lifted.

"Then there aren't any lines to learn!" Kitty said. She took a happy slurp out of her limeade until the straw grumbled at the bottom of the glass.

"Why not do the whole lot of it that way?" Darbie said to Sophie. "We might take our turns narrating and the rest could be in pantomime."

"No offense, Darbie," Fiona said. "But we don't do our films that way."

"But this isn't the flicks," Darbie said.

"Does that mean movies?" Kitty said.

"Yes."

"I like that. Let's start calling our movies the 'flicks'!"

"Would you please stay on task?" Fiona snapped at her, pen jittering on the table. "Now we only have three and a *half* days to get this done."

"All the more reason to do it in narration and pantomime," Darbie said.

Fiona looked at Sophie, shaking her head. "Explain it to her, would you, Soph? You're, like, the only one she understands."

Sophie reached for the end of her hair to make a mustache, and then tossed it over her shoulder. "I like the idea," she said. "I can just see it in my mind."

"Well, the rest of us can't," Fiona said.

"I can," Kitty said. "Darbie, do you think you have any more of that limeade stuff?"

"Kit-teee!" Fiona said.

"This is a class idea!" Darbie said. "I'll fetch us some more to drink."

When Kitty had skipped off after Darbie, Fiona stared hard at Sophie.

"Why are you letting her be the boss of everything?" Fiona said. "You're the director, and she's usurping your authority."

Okay, so that was one Sophie hadn't heard before. "I don't think I AM the director this time," Sophie said. "This is Darbie's story, so she knows more about it than we do."

Fiona yanked her hair out of her face. "She has never made a film before—or done any acting at all, I bet. You have to take control if she starts to mess this up, Sophie—or we'll never beat the Corn Pops."

"She won't make a bags of it! And besides, that's not why—"

"Come here, you guys!" Kitty squealed from down the hall. "Darbie's got posters we can use and everything! This is going to be way cool!"

It WAS cool. Darbie's uncle had signs that had actually been on walls during "the Troubles"—saying things like "Disband the RUC," whatever that meant. There was so much Sophie still didn't understand about the Troubles. They also had pictures of Darbie's old school and house in Northern Ireland so they could set up the stage exactly the way it was for each scene. Fiona argued that it would take too much time changing furniture every other minute, but Sophie and Darbie figured out a way to use the same few chairs and one table for every scene and just change things like flowers in a vase or a pile of schoolbooks. Aunt Emily told them she was impressed. She said she did some theater when she was in college, and that's exactly what they used to do.

So it only seemed to make sense that Darbie and Sophie would write the script and hand the scenes to Fiona and Kitty to figure out what Aunt Emily called the "set changes." Sophie told them to be sure to talk in the new theater language Aunt Emily was teaching them.

Kitty was amazingly good at it. Sophie couldn't tell whether Fiona was or not because she spent most of the time scowling at the Treasure Book while she wrote things down. Still, by Saturday afternoon the whole script was written, which meant they didn't have to meet on Sunday.

But Saturday night, Darbie called and asked Sophie if she could come over the next day anyway and make sure everything was perfect before they handed it in to Miss Blythe on Monday.

That day was Sophie's favorite day of work—because as she and Darbie took turns reading the narration and walking through the scenes of pantomime, it all became real.

Sophie clutched at her chest as she hid behind a "counter" in a chipper—a fish and chips shop—being little Darbie, while angry men dragged the owner out into the street, yelling at him because he wasn't welcome in the neighborhood.

She felt a lump in her throat as she waved good-bye to her ma, who was going off to another peace talk someplace far away.

And she cried real tears as she put flowers next to a "headstone" on that same ma's grave.

"You *have* to play me when we perform this, Sophie," Darbie said—handing Sophie a box of Kleenex. "I can't even be me like you can!"

"Then you have to play your ma," Sophie said. "Because you're the only one who can make me cry like that."

That would mean, of course, that Kitty and Fiona would take turns reading and playing all the other parts.

"Fiona won't fancy that," Darbie said.

"You mean she won't like it?" Sophie said. "She'll love it! She's very versatile—you know, like she can play any role." Sophie nodded thoughtfully at the script. "We should have her put more big words in the narration too."

Darbie agreed. Fiona didn't.

Before school on Monday, Sophie told Fiona everything as the four of them half ran down the hall to find Miss Blythe.

"You don't have time to do it before we give it to her right now," Sophie said breathlessly. "But you can do it later."

"What if I don't want to do it at all?" Fiona said. She slowed to a walk, so that Sophie had to cut back her pace too. She stared at Fiona.

"Why not?" Sophie said.

"Because it's not my script," Fiona said. "It's yours and Darbie's. And now you want me to come in and fix it for you so you'll sound smarter."

Sophie squinted at her. "I don't get it."

Fiona rolled her eyes and sighed and shook her head.

"It's so obvious, Sophie," she said. "If you don't know, I'm sure not going to tell you."

Sophie couldn't get her mouth to move. She was still just gawking at Fiona, as Darbie would say, when Kitty and Darbie ran back to them. Kitty jumped right up on Fiona's back, piggy back style.

"We gave it to Miss Blythe!" she said, arms locked around Fiona's neck.

"She's going to love it, so she is!" Darbie said. It was the first time Sophie had ever heard a giggle in Darbie's voice.

Fiona shook Kitty from her back and kept her eyes on Sophie. "If she doesn't," she said, "don't expect me to fix it."

As it turned out, Miss Blythe didn't think it needed "fixing" at all. She sailed right over to their group's table in arts class with the script and went on and on about the creativity and the sensitivity and every other "ivity" they had managed to get in there, all the while squiggling her fingers in the air with punctuation marks Sophie had never seen before.

Kitty and Darbie beamed. Fiona sulked. Sophie closed her eyes and tried to imagine Jesus so she could beg him for an answer to this new mess.

It seems like I just get one thing worked out, she said to him in her mind, *and something else goes wrong. Now what do I do?*

She peeked at Fiona, who was still looking at Miss Blythe with lead in her eyes.

And why is Fiona making this so hard?

Sophie wanted to drag her out into the hallway and eat the head off her, as Darbie would say. That's how mad she was.

It was hard to keep from showing that over the next three days as the group rehearsed. Darbie told Sophie that Fiona had a "right puss on her, she did," but Sophie was determined not to let Fiona's pouting spoil their presentation. Every time Fiona shrugged when they asked for her opinion, or read the narration like a first grader in a reading group, or walked through a scene as if she were a stick instead of a "bitter peeler"—the Irish term for policeman—Sophie just chewed at her lip and kept going.

Until Wednesday, just three days before the performance. And then she couldn't hold it back any longer.

Nine

✳ ⌂ ❀

The group was rehearsing that Wednesday after school at Darbie's, using her back deck as the stage. They had all their tables and chairs—their set pieces, Aunt Emily told them—and the small stuff like flowers and teacups—their props, Aunt Emily said—everything lined up perfectly backstage. There was a copy of the script for each of them, and they were even wearing their costumes. They wore blue jeans and white T-shirts so they could put other things on top—aprons and hats and Sophie's black velvet cape, which she wore as Darbie going to her ma's gravestone. Kitty had surprised them with that scathingly brilliant idea.

Everything would have been perfect—except that Fiona was being such the Puss Face, as Darbie whispered to Sophie, that she would hardly speak to anyone, and when she did, every word squeezed out between her teeth like the last of the glue coming out of the tube.

"The audience won't be able to hear you if you don't talk louder," Sophie said during one of Fiona's tight-jawed narrations.

"I don't see any audience," Fiona said.

"There will be one," Sophie said. "We have to pretend they're there."

"They'll all be asleep anyway," Fiona said. "So what difference does it make?"

Over on stage left Kitty's forehead puckered up. "Why will they be asleep?"

"They won't," Sophie said. She looked hard at Fiona. "Let's do that part again."

It was that way all through rehearsal, which made it hard for Sophie to concentrate on being Darbie. Instead of imagining that the wadded-up brown lunch bags Fiona and Kitty were throwing were stones being pelted at Darbie by mean kids, she saw the Fruit Loops drooling and snoring in the back of the room and the Corn Pops dozing off nearby. *The audience wouldn't go to sleep if YOU weren't so boring!* she wanted to shout at Fiona. The way Fiona walked around all stiff during the throw-rocks-at-Darbie scene made Kitty act like a robot too.

But at least Darbie's giving it her best, Sophie thought. During the part where Darbie's mother died on the street next to her smashed car with Darbie/Sophie at her side, Darbie touched Sophie's face like a real mother would, and Sophie burst into tears.

"That'll wake the audience up," Fiona said. "They'll be guffawing all over the place."

Darbie sat straight up and glared at her. "What does that mean?"

"Throwing up?" Kitty said.

Fiona shook her head. "Laughing themselves into oblivion. That is so corny."

"Her mother died!" Sophie said. "I'm supposed to cry!"

"It sounds fake," Fiona said. She studied her fingernails. "I think we should take that scene out. We need to get some humor in."

"Humor!" Sophie said.

She could feel Darbie stiffening beside her. "What's such a gas about this?"

"That means 'what's funny,'" Sophie said.

"Nothing," Fiona said. "That's the point. The Corn Pops are going to be entertaining the audience. We're going to be making them wish they were having a tooth pulled or something."

"We'll entertain them too!" Sophie said. Looking up, she could see right up Fiona's flaring nostrils.

"Right," Fiona said. "They'll be laughing at us."

"Will they, Sophie?" Kitty said.

"No, they will not." Sophie's words came out as squeezed-tight as Fiona's. "Not unless Fiona keeps on making a bags of it."

"Acting the maggot," Darbie mumbled.

"I knew it," Fiona squeezed back at Sophie. "I knew you would turn all this into my fault. But I'm not the one. I didn't have anything to do with this. You and Darbie planned it all, and then you're all telling me and Kitty what to do!" Fiona shoved her hair out of her face with the side of her hand. "I'm so not your little slave. If you don't start listening to me, I'm going to find another group to be in. And don't think I won't!"

She planted her hands on her hips and lowered her face so that she was slitting her eyes right into Sophie's like a pair of knives. Sophie felt her own slashing back.

"You're being selfish, Fiona," she said. "We're doing this for Darbie—not for you!"

There was a stinging silence. Somewhere in the middle of it, Fiona tore her script into confetti and stormed into the house. Nobody followed her.

After a few minutes, Aunt Emily came out, mouth in a grim line, and suggested they call it a day and let everybody cool off. Kitty looked more than happy to escape.

"I don't think this was a good idea at all, Sophie," Darbie said when Kitty was gone. She tucked her swingy hair behind both ears, and Sophie could see a red rim forming around each eye.

"It's the best idea ever," Sophie said. "It's class. I just don't think Fiona gets what we're trying to do."

Darbie pulled her lips into a thin line, the way a grown-up would. "If she doesn't, nobody will."

"Then we totally have to do it so they all will." She knew she was sounding like Kitty, but there was no other way to sound. She felt so much younger than Darbie all of a sudden.

"I won't be made to look like an eejit," Darbie said. Her eyes went hard as stones. "I'll take a bad grade before I'll be laughed at."

Sophie opened her mouth—and then she closed it again, because now she couldn't promise Darbie that the entire audience wouldn't fall right out of their chairs.

Aunt Emily invited Sophie to stay for supper, and she and Darbie's uncle Patrick spent the whole time, as far as Sophie was concerned, turning themselves inside out to make the girls laugh. But the last thing Sophie wanted to do was "guffaw."

By the time Aunt Emily took her home, Mama and Daddy had already left for a meeting at church, and Zeke was asleep. Sophie curled up on her bed and tried to sort out whether to imagine Colleen O'Bravo, get Jesus in her mind, or just camp outside Mama and Daddy's bedroom door until they got home and beg them to let her see Dr. Peter. She was ready to try all three when Lacie tapped on the door and let herself in before Sophie could even tell her to go away.

"I am so bored!" Lacie said as she sprawled across Sophie's bed just like she'd done every day since she'd been grounded.

"Make yourself at home," Sophie said in a dry voice.

"I've done all my homework. I've studied for my geography test twelve times. I've written letters to everybody I ever knew in Houston—I mean letters—not even email. You'd think they'd at least let me get on the Internet."

"No, you wouldn't," Sophie said. "You're grounded."

"Really, Einstein?" Lacie sighed. "So what are you doing?"

Sophie pulled her script out of her backpack. "I'm trying to figure out what to do about our play."

"Another film?" Lacie said. "I don't know what you'd do if you had real problems."

"I do!" Sophie said. "This is for a school project. Everybody's parents are going to be there, and if Fiona doesn't get her act together, I'm going to have to transfer to another school or something."

"Let me see that, Drama Queen," Lacie said. She snatched the script from Sophie's hand.

"If you're going to make me feel like an eejit, I will eat the head off you."

"Whatever that means." Lacie moved her eyes across the page. Sophie flopped back against her pillows and tried to think what Colleen O'Bravo would do if she had a sister. She didn't, of course. She was an orphan without siblings, ever since the Troubles—

"Huh," Lacie said.

"Just give it back," Sophie said. She stuck her hand out, but Lacie waved her away, her eyes still glued to the page.

"Who wrote this?" Lacie said.

"I did—well, Darbie and I did. She's Irish."

"Is this like her story or something?" Lacie said.

"Yes—which is why I don't want you laughing at it. All those things really happened to her."

"Dude—it's horrible."

"It isn't horrible! Miss Blythe said it was a good script—"

"I'm not talking about the script—I'm talking about what happened to this Darbie chick. How could a person go through something like that?" Lacie turned the page and after a moment she looked up at Sophie, who was now breathing like the spin cycle on the washing machine. "This is good, Soph. You sure you guys didn't have somebody helping you?"

"Yes," Sophie said. She felt a smile starting to form, and then she scowled up at the ceiling. "I wish Fiona thought it was good. She says we're going to get laughed out of the school."

"I guess it could get cheesy when you act it out," Lacie said.

"Only if *she* keeps acting like she hates it," Sophie said. "She's supposed to be my best friend, and she's being all stupid and making a bags of the whole thing and messing everything up. Darbie doesn't deserve that."

"Did I miss the part where you started speaking another language?" Lacie tossed the script on the bedspread and turned on her side, cheek in hand as she leaned on her elbow. "Okay—let me get this straight. You and Darbie wrote the script. You spent all day Sunday at Darbie's house. You ate dinner at Darbie's house tonight. But Fiona's your best friend."

"Yeah," Sophie said. "So?"

"Du-uh!" Lacie said. "It doesn't take a genius to figure out that Fiona's feeling left out because you're paying all this attention to Darbie. Get a clue, Soph."

"But we already went through this with Maggie when we were doing our science project! Fiona knows I can be friends with other people and still be her best friend."

"But back then, every other word that came out of your mouth wasn't 'Maggie.' Besides, you and Maggie and Fiona and—what's that little whiny child's name?"

"Kitty."

"Ya'll are all friends with each other. How does Irish Girl fit in?"

Sophie considered that as she poked at a tiny hole in the bedspread. "Darbie likes Fiona okay—but I think she knows Fiona doesn't like her that much."

Lacie sat up, legs crossed in front of her. "Okay, so two things are different. One—you didn't spend every spare minute with Maggie and leave Fiona out, and two—Maggie was part of the group, and Darbie isn't. She's not a—what do you guys call yourselves?"

"Corn Flakes."

Sophie's throat felt thick, and it was hard to breathe. She hadn't meant to hurt Fiona, but the way Lacie described it Sophie might as well have punched her best friend in the heart.

"Fiona probably hates me now!" she said.

Lacie put up both hands. "Okay, don't go flipping out on me. For once in your life, listen to a little advice from me—hello, I've been there."

Sophie doubted that, but she nodded. Anything to keep from losing Fiona, which was suddenly more important than the showcase or Colleen O'Bravo or even her video camera.

"Look," Lacie said, "you have to make Fiona feel like she's important again."

"The only way to do that is to drop Darbie," Sophie said.

"Are you going to listen to me or what?"

Sophie gave her another glum nod.

"You call Fiona up and tell her she's your best friend in the world and you want to hear why she thinks the script is lame."

"But it isn't."

"No, duh. But just listen to her and make her feel like you're taking it all in—and then you tell her she's the only one who can make it work."

"That's not true."

"Sure it is. If she keeps 'making bags out of it' or whatever, it is going to bomb. You said that yourself."

Sophie squinted through her glasses. "You think that'll work?"

"Trust me. Do it right now. I'll get the phone—at least that'll give me an excuse to hold it in my hand. I'm going into telephone withdrawal. I'm going to forget how to use one."

Before Sophie could even think about it, Lacie punched in Fiona's number and handed the phone to Sophie.

"I'll stay here in case you need any coaching," Lacie said. "Hold it out so I can hear."

You really are bored, Sophie thought. But for the first time since Fiona had ripped up her script, Sophie felt a little sparkle of hope. When Fiona answered the phone, she launched right in.

But before she could even get out the words, "I am so sorry about what happened this afternoon"—with Lacie nodding at her side—Fiona said, "Stop. Just stop."

"I was just—" Sophie said.

"If it's about the showcase thing, don't waste your time."

"But I really want to hear—"

"Forget it," Fiona said. "The Corn Pops still need another dancer. I'm auditioning for them tomorrow."

"No!" Sophie said.

Lacie put her fingers in her ears.

"I don't care if everybody laughs at me when I'm just being my weird self," Fiona said. "But I don't want them laughing if I'm doing something totally lame that isn't me. Besides—"

There was a pause. Lacie nudged Sophie.

"What?" Sophie said. "It doesn't have to be lame—I want to hear your ideas."

"I can't get a bad grade," Fiona said. "I'm the one who made sure you got good grades so you could have your camera. But now that you don't listen to me, you're going down. And I'm not going down with you."

It was abruptly silent. When a dull drone sounded in Sophie's ear, Lacie took the phone from her and pushed the button.

"She hung up, Soph," she said. "She just flat hung up on you."

Ten

Sophie stared at the phone, which was still in Lacie's hand.

"That was just wrong," Lacie said, flipping her ponytail. "If she's going to be that way about it, you don't need her for a friend."

"No—I do!" Sophie said. "It's all my fault!"

Lacie shook her head, but when the sound of Mama and Daddy coming through the kitchen made its way up the stairs, she was out the door in mid-shake.

"What happened?" Sophie heard her call down over the banister.

"We need to talk," Daddy called back up.

Sophie felt herself folding in as she got up and closed her door. *There goes another hour or two,* she thought.

In fact, it wasn't even a minute or two before Lacie was bellowing, "I don't want to go to another church! You're taking me away from my friends! I'm the middle school youth group president!"

Colleen O'Bravo perched the green hat atop her head and crumpled beneath its brim. "She'll eat the heads off of them for sure," she said to herself. "And it will not do a bit of good. When Ma and Da make up their minds—"

Sophie's thoughts trailed off. Colleen wasn't much help right now. Sophie was losing her best friend, and it was going to take more than imagination to get her back.

"I want Dr. Peter!" she whispered to the walls.

What would he say? She closed her eyes and pictured him on the window seat in his office, face pillow in hand, squinting through his glasses with twinkly blue eyes.

I read the Bible story, Sophie said to him in her mind. *And it helped me with Darbie. But Fiona—*

She could see Dr. Peter wrinkling his nose, pushing up his glasses. *No 'But Fiona,' Loodle*, he would say. *It's in the Bible. It's truth. Love her the way Jesus loves his friends.*

Sophie was about to kick her feet—rather than even think about washing them or anybody else's—when the phone jangled beside her. She snatched it up, the word "Fiona!" already on her lips.

But it was Darbie, jabbering like the words couldn't come out fast enough. "You haven't a clue who just called me! It was Fiona—and she reefed me!"

Sophie didn't even have to ask if that was the same as eating the head off her.

"She told me she was going to audition for the Corny Pops," Darbie went on. "Now what are we going to do? We'll surely make a bags of doing our show without her! This is desperate!"

"You know it!" Sophie said. "We have to get her back is all—I know you'll hate this idea, but I'm trying to figure out how I'm supposed to love her like Jesus. What I mean is—"

"I know all about that," Darbie said.

"You do?" Sophie said.

"Don't be thinking it isn't hard to love some blaggard who's just left your garden in flitters bolting through with his evil signs—or worse. I'm quite the expert on doing what the Lord says even when you'd rather be hanged. I've been doing it for ages."

Sophie sat up straighter on the bed. "You mean, like washing people's feet, sort of?"

"I know that story. And the one about the lady who wiped Jesus' feet with her *hair*."

Sophie barely took time to notice that Darbie pronounced Jesus, "Jaysus." She could only gawk at the phone.

"My ma and me, we always talked about the Bible stories—we would never have been able to carry on without them." Darbie's voice dropped. "My aunt and uncle don't go to church—and it's murder without it."

Sophie finally found her voice, and it came out squeaky-nervous. "You know the foot-washing story then?"

"I do."

"Well—we have to love Fiona like that. You know, wash her feet. Only I don't know how."

"It isn't difficult," Darbie said. "Bowl. Towel. Water."

"You mean, really wash her feet?" Sophie said. Her voice was squealing up into dog-world.

"That's what the story says. And you know what else it says, of course."

"No," Sophie said.

"Fetch your Bible, then," Darbie said.

But before Sophie could even reach for hers, the door opened and Daddy stuck his head in. The skin under his eyes was long. "Lights out, Soph," he said. "We'll talk tomorrow. Deal?"

Sophie nodded. When the door closed, she whispered to Darbie, "I have to go."

"Read the entire story," Darbie whispered back. "The part where he gives out to them—you know, gets in their faces, as you Americans say. Sometimes that's love too, my ma always told me, mostly when she was giving out to me about something I did wrong. Oh—and I'll bring the pitcher tomorrow."

"For what?" Sophie said.

"For the water. And let's do it in the corner of the play yard. I don't fancy having every eejit in the school gawking at us."

Sophie's mind was whirling when she hung up, but she reached for her Bible and her flashlight and tented herself under the covers.

Jesus loved them by getting in their faces? Sophie thought. *Sounds like something Daddy would say*—"Soph, I'm doing this for your own good."

Chewing at her hair, Sophie read the story three more times, searching for a place where Jesus—how had Darbie said it?—gave out to the disciples.

Okay, so I'm Luke, she thought, *and Jesus is being all nice and washing everybody's feet, and then he gets in our faces*. Sophie sat up and pretended that Jesus was back at his place at the table, leaning across to talk to them all. Sophie/Luke squinted back to see him. Jesus' voice was getting firmer; it was as if she could almost press her hand against his words.

"I tell you the truth," he said, "no servant is greater than his master, nor is a messenger greater than the one who sent him. Now that you know these things, you will be blessed if you do them."

Sophie tried to hear it again, with Jesus using an even sterner voice, like he wanted to make sure they got it. She couldn't quite remember the exact words. In her head it was, "If you understand what I'm saying to you, then act like it."

Sophie/Luke scrunched up his face as he tried to get it. As always, his teacher's eyes were kind even though he was stern, and he felt himself breathing deep in his chest. *He expects me to love and love and love some more*, Sophie/Luke thought. *He* watched the faces of his friends glow in the half darkness. The Master Jesus was telling them what they had to do. But he wasn't getting all yelly and making them feel like—eejits. "This is what I have to do," Sophie/Luke told himself. "I have to make people understand, only with love."

By then, Sophie's eyes felt sandy, and she burrowed farther under the bedspread with the flashlight still in her hand.

Darbie knows about "Jaysus" too, she thought as she fell asleep. *What a CLASS discovery.*

Mama didn't even question why Sophie wanted to borrow a bowl and a towel to take to school. She bagged them up so Sophie could carry them on the bus without bopping anybody in the head, and as Sophie went for the door she said to her, "I'm sorry we haven't been much help to you, Dream Girl. But Daddy and I are going to make special time for you tonight."

As good as that sounded, Sophie couldn't think about it right then. She met Darbie at school just as Aunt Emily was dropping her off, and they waited like crouched tigers for Maggie and Kitty to appear. Sophie knew Fiona would be the last one to get there since, without a nanny, it was probably a zoo at her house in the mornings. That was fine, because it took a few minutes to explain the foot washing to Kitty and Maggie.

"I don't get it," Maggie said, her voice flat. "What if her feet aren't dirty?"

"It isn't about dirt," Sophie said patiently. "It's about showing Fiona that I love her and I respect her, but she can't just go off and pout."

Maggie shrugged. "So why don't you just tell her?"

"I tried that," Sophie said—less patiently. "She wouldn't listen—but this will get her attention."

"How do you know?" Maggie said.

Darbie gave a soft grunt. "Wouldn't it get yours?"

"I think it sounds cool!" Kitty said. "Will you do mine?"

"Fiona first," Sophie said.

"Since she's the one bolting off to join up with the Pop Corns," Darbie said.

Kitty would have died of the giggles if the Buntings' black SUV hadn't squealed up to the front of the school just then.

"Go out to your places, okay?" Sophie said.

Sophie hurried to grab Fiona the second her foot emerged from the car. Fiona slammed the door against the chaos inside the vehicle and tried to wriggle past her.

"No way," Sophie said to her as she dragged her away from the car door. "I'm going to love you whether you like it or not."

Somehow Sophie got her to the play yard, where the other girls were kneeling in the far corner, their backs to the rest of the Great Marsh Elementary world.

"I don't have time for this," Fiona said. They were the first words she'd spoken. "I have to go audition."

"You have to do this first," Sophie said. She hoped her eyes were Jesus-kind, because her voice was coming out in a very UN-Jesus way. He would never sound like a mom about to smack her kids in the cookie aisle at the Farm Fresh.

"Sit," Maggie said to Fiona when she and Sophie got to the corner. She pointed to a folded-up jacket placed on the ground for her bum.

Sophie sucked in a breath, but Fiona took a seat. *Good thing she can't resist a mystery*, Sophie thought.

Sophie got on her knees facing Fiona while Darbie poured water from the pitcher into the bowl and Kitty and Maggie took off Fiona's shoes—with only a halfway protest from Fiona. Sophie took off her jean jacket and wrapped a big beach towel around her waist.

"I get it," Fiona said. "You're going to stick my foot in that water—although why I can't even fathom."

"Because I love you, that's why," Sophie said. She cradled Fiona's heel in her palm and she could see her own hands shaking. Her voice was barely coming out at all. She was sure Jesus hadn't been this scared that it wasn't going to work.

"I want to serve you," Sophie said. "Not yell at you and make you feel left out." She leaned down and swept some water over Fiona's toes. "You're my best friend and I really want to hear your ideas."

Fiona seemed to be staring at the water bubbles. She didn't say a word.

"I'm sorry too," Darbie said. "It was diabolical of me not to consider your feelings."

"That must mean really terrible," Kitty muttered to Maggie.

Sophie pulled Fiona's feet out of the bowl and rested them on the towel across her lap. "Please don't go join up with the Corn Pops," she said as she dried between Fiona's toes. "We need you. I'll be a better friend, I promise."

Fiona finally looked up at her, forehead bunched into folds. "I don't know," she said.

"What's not to know?" Maggie said. "She apologized. She said she wants to serve you. Now you accept and it's done."

"Just because she washed my feet?" Fiona said.

"Can you ever stop being a hard chaw?" Darbie said. "She's groveling for you, and you're wanting more! I never saw such an ungrateful—"

"Don't yell!" Kitty said, just before she burst into tears.

"You sound like the Corn Pops," Maggie said. "I get enough of this at rehearsal."

"Maybe I'll just go be a Corn Pop!" Fiona said. "At least I know how they feel about me."

"Are you gone in the head?" Darbie said. "Sophie just told you—"

"Just stop! Everybody STOP!" Sophie's voice practically squeaked out of her ears as she struggled to her feet. The bowl turned over, and the water hurried toward the fence in rivulets. Nobody even looked at it. "We're the Corn Flakes," she said when they were quiet. "We take care of each other's feelings. And that means everybody. We don't act like this. Now just—stop."

She snatched up her jacket and hugged it around her, but she knew her shivers weren't from the cold. Even her voice was shaky as she said, "This is what we have to do. We have to stop fighting and we have to work together. If we don't, we're going to mess up our whole showcase—and the whole Corn Flakes."

"Nuh-uh!" Kitty said.

"Yuh-huh," Maggie said. "The Corn Pops' dance is, like, professional, but right now they can hardly stand each other."

"You don't even know how lucky you are to have friends like you do," Darbie said. "I had to leave all mine behind." She straightened her shoulders. "I can go off my nut sometimes, but I'll try not to eat the head off anyone again—you have my word."

Kitty whimpered. Sophie thought she said something like, "Pleeeeze, Fiona."

Fiona flipped her hair out of her face and looked at Maggie. "So the Corn Pops' dance is spectacular, huh?"

"They'll win," Maggie said.

For the first time in what felt to Sophie like centuries, Fiona's gray eyes flickered with interest. Her mouth came unbunched, and she gave a little bow of a smile. "Oh, no, they will *not* win," she said. She turned to Darbie. "Okay—it's over. No more fighting. We are going to make this the BEST performance that ever was. Whatever it takes."

Darbie blinked for a second. "All right, then. Fair play," she said. Her voice was careful. "After school at my house? No foostering about?"

"No foostering," Fiona said. "I'm serious."

"I won't fooster, either," Kitty said.

The bell rang, and Maggie and Kitty and Darbie picked up the remains of the foot washing. Fiona tucked her arm through Sophie's and steered her toward the building.

Sophie felt strangely stiff beside her. Fiona had said she wanted to win the showcase — beat the Corn Pops. But that wasn't really the mission. Besides that, Fiona had never said she was sorry.

"Boppa says I'm insecure and I need to get over it," Fiona said. Her voice was sunny, as if they had not had a shouting match just five minutes before. "I guess I shouldn't have told you that I was going to audition for the Corn Pops. I called Julia and set it up, but I was never really going to do it. Boppa about ate the head off me when he heard me on the phone with her."

Then I washed your feet for nothing? Sophie wanted to say. She felt herself going even more rigid.

"You know what, Soph?" Fiona said.

Sophie shook her head.

"Sometimes I really want to know how you can be so good all the time." She pulled Sophie's arm closer. "I'm glad we're okay again."

Sophie nodded — but she wondered if they really were.

216

Eleven

Just as Darbie and Fiona had both promised, there were no more "ructions," as Darbie called them, while the group worked during every possible second on Thursday and Friday to make their play the best thing anyone had ever seen—at least at Great Marsh Elementary. It seemed to make Darbie happy that they were finally doing justice to her life story, and Kitty, of course, was happy because everybody else was happy.

But Sophie still had an unsettled feeling inside her about Fiona. Even during her special time with Mama and Daddy on Thursday night, while they ate yogurt and Mama's homemade granola in the kitchen, she couldn't quite explain it.

"All Fiona wants to do is win," she told them, "and our mission is to make people understand how horrible it can be if they fight and are violent—you know, like in Northern Ireland."

Daddy pulled his upper half out of the refrigerator, holding a can of whipped cream. "Why can't you do both?" he said. "Win and educate at the same time."

"Besides," Mama said, "I think it's what you and the other Corn Flakes are learning from all this that's really important. You're really being mature."

Daddy squirted a tall pile of whipped cream on his granola-topped yogurt and finished with a dot on Sophie's nose. "You're a winner no matter what happens, Soph. I wish it was this easy with your sister right now."

Sophie soaked that in for a second, waiting for a warm feeling to fill her up. But being praised over Lacie didn't do it for her like she'd always dreamed it would.

"We're changing churches, aren't we?" she said.

"We are," Mama said. "But I think it's going to be a good thing."

"Lacie doesn't think so."

"Right now, Lacie doesn't think — period." Daddy shook the whipped cream can again. "You don't look like you're about to pitch a fit over it though, Soph. I appreciate that."

"I don't have friends there like she does," Sophie said.

"You will at our new church. At least one." Mama grinned at Daddy. "Should I tell her?"

"Nah — make her beg."

"Da-ad!" Sophie snatched up the can and pointed it in his direction.

His hands flew up. "I'll tell you anything you want to know. Just don't shoot."

"Who's at the new church that I know?" Sophie said.

"A cute little man with glasses," Mama said. "He teaches Bible study to your age group."

"Dr. Peter?" Sophie said. "Go way outta that!"

"It's not a bit of a horse's hoof. I'm telling you the truth."

Daddy looked from one of them to the other, a mustache of whipped cream under his nose. "Why don't I understand a thing you women are saying?" he said.

Mama patted his arm. "You'd have to have a bit of the Irish in you," she said.

On Friday during arts class, each group went into the caf-eteria-turned-auditorium to do its presentation privately for Miss Blythe, so she could make sure they were ready for a real audience. Sophie's group was scheduled to go last.

"Miss Blythe is saving the best for the end," Fiona whispered as they waited, dry-mouthed, backstage with their set pieces and props.

"She wants a dramatic finish," Darbie said.

"I have to go to the bathroom," Kitty said.

Sophie put her hands out and the Corn Flakes and Darbie grabbed on, and Sophie prayed. "Help us do what you did, Jesus, and that's help people understand."

"And please help us win," Fiona said.

"Amen," Kitty said.

"Are you ready, actors?' Miss Blythe called from in front of the stage.

Sophie tried to brush away the nagging Fiona-thought and gave Kitty a little push to go out and start the narration.

"Let's do it perfect," Fiona said.

"Perfect" didn't totally describe their performance for Miss Blythe. Kitty lost her place twice when she was reading the narration, and Fiona forgot to put out a chair for one of the scenes, and Sophie couldn't quite get the tears out at the "graveside." But when they were finished, Miss Blythe stood up and shouted, "Bravo! Brav-O!"

"I bet she didn't do that for the Corn Pops," Fiona whispered. Sophie could see the triumphant gleam in her eyes even in the dark behind the curtain. Sophie felt a bit victorious her-self. Maybe, like Daddy said, they could educate AND win.

And then she looked at Darbie, who was twisting her mouth up as she looked at Fiona, like she was trying not to say out loud what she was thinking. But Sophie knew what it was. Fiona herself still didn't get it yet. Was there any chance that the other kids would?

It was hard, though, on Saturday not to think about the possibility of the entire audience standing up, calling out "Bravo!" The more the cheers and applause went through Sophie's head, the more she dreamed that the stage curtains were going to open up to the Corn Flakes' secret world, and other kids were finally going to understand about how stupid it was to hate and fight. She tried not to let herself add in a vision of herself accepting first prize with her fellow cast members and waving to Mama and Daddy in the front row and seeing them beam with pride. But that seemed to be the ONLY thing Fiona could think about.

She called four times on Saturday, just to assure Sophie that they were so going to blow everyone else away. Darbie called twice to ask Sophie to convince her that things were going to be "quite different" after their performance, what with the Corn Pops and Fruit Loops no longer "acting the maggot" because they would now be educated. She was still having trouble believing it. Kitty called only once, and Sophie couldn't tell whether she was giggling or crying. She was definitely Kitty-nervous.

Sophie wasn't very nervous—not with Daddy having flowers delivered to the house for her, and Mama fixing her an herbal bath and playing Irish music while she French-braided Sophie's hair, and even Lacie coming out of her church misery long enough to give her a card that said, "I'm actually kind of proud of you. Go figure." That all made it easier to push her Fiona misgivings aside and think only of Miss Blythe predicting more bravos.

When she got to the arts room that night, she couldn't hear Miss Blythe saying ANYTHING over the chaos that ruled.

The Fruit Loops were grabbing the soccer balls the Wheaties were using in their performance and using them to play keep-away over the heads of the Corn Pops, who were all trying to get their hair buns to look exactly the same. Willoughby's hair was so short and wavy it kept popping out like Slinkies all over her scalp.

Maggie stood in the midst of the Corn Pops, zipping up zippers and adjusting tights.

"They can't even put their pantyhose on right?" Fiona said when Sophie joined her group in the corner.

"They're a bit thick, those four girls are," Darbie said.

Just then Anne-Stuart marched up to Maggie and said her sequined top was itchy, followed by B.J. complaining that her satin shorts made her look fat.

"Those costumes are quite grand," Darbie said. "I don't see what they're raving on about."

"Of course they're grand," Kitty said, tilting her chin up. "Our Maggie made them."

"One thing is for sure," Fiona said. "They are so not going to get a good grade for getting along and being organized. But look at us, all sitting here ready to go."

Sophie glanced over in time to see the victorious gleam still in Fiona's eyes.

Meanwhile, Miss Blythe's hands were punctuating the air with flying exclamation points, and her usually silken hair was looking electrified.

"She's going off her nut," Darbie said.

Kitty giggled. And giggled. And kept giggling until she got the hiccups and had to dart to the restroom before she wet her pants.

"That can't be good," Darbie said.

"Don't worry," Fiona said. "I've got Kitty handled. Besides, she's not freaking out as bad as Willoughby. Look at her."

Willoughby did appear to be losing control. Her head was by now a mass of springs, which were bobbing to and fro as she looked from one scolding Corn Pop to another. They were taking turns putting their noses close to hers and all but chewing her lips off. She finally sat down on the floor, green sequins and all, and bawled like a baby calf.

Miss Blythe did manage to get everyone settled down and explained that they would all sit in the back of the cafeteria during the showcase to watch the other groups perform until it was their group's time to go on. The Corn Flakes grabbed each other's hands and squeezed.

"This is class," Darbie said. "They'll all of them see us, they will."

"See us win," Fiona said.

See us completing our mission, Sophie wanted to say. But Miss Blythe was already swearing them to silence and leading them down the hall toward the cafeteria. Sophie clung to Fiona's hand with her own clammy one and followed.

The cafeteria was festooned with giant shamrocks and green streamers, and every chair was filled with somebody's mom or dad or grandma. Sophie stood on her tiptoes to find Mama and Daddy, who had the video camera in his hand—and Lacie and Zeke, right in front of Boppa's bald head. Fiona's dad was there too, but not her mom, and Sophie felt sad for Fiona—until she spotted another familiar face, twinkling behind wire-rimmed glasses.

"Dr. Peter's here!" she hissed to Fiona.

"No way!"

Sophie tried to point him out, but the lights went off—amid squeals from the sixth-grade class—and Miss Blythe appeared on the stage, hair once again hanging calmly in silky furls. Sophie sucked in a breath she couldn't let go of.

Are we just going to, like, wash everybody's feet when we're doing this? she thought.

Colleen O'Bravo nodded her red ringlets.

Jesus looked at her firmly and kindly.

Sophie LaCroix settled back in her seat and breathed out a long, praying breath.

Most of the groups' presentations were good, especially the Wheaties', who did creative ball passing with feet, heads, and hips, all to music. Even the Fruit Loops were decent, Sophie had to admit. They did a karate demonstration, complete with a lot of loud noises that Fiona whispered weren't necessary. Still, Sophie clapped for them when they took their bows.

And then the Corn Pops performed.

They filled the stage with their green sparkly costumes and glittered hair bows and silver pom-poms and did a routine that was a dance and a cheer and a gymnastics program all kicked and bounced and wiggled into one. Sophie truly thought she was watching something on TV.

Julia could kick her leg so high her foot nearly hit the top of her head.

Anne-Stuart executed one perfect split after another.

B.J.'s cartwheels were as smooth as her satin shorts.

And Willoughby did so many spritely little backflips it made Sophie dizzy.

When they struck their final poses, the whole audience stood up and cheered and whistled and clapped their hands over their heads. Everybody except Fiona.

"It wasn't THAT good," she whispered to Sophie from her seat. "Wait 'til they see ours."

"Come on then," Darbie said, nodding over at Miss Blythe, who was motioning to them from the stage. Sophie could almost see question marks popping out of the teacher's head. "We're on."

It was as if someone had turned a dial in Sophie, making everything go faster than normal speed. They were backstage checking their props and set pieces that Aunt Emily had put in place for them before the show. They were huddled behind the curtain listening to Miss Blythe introduce them with exclamation points in her voice. The lights were on and Kitty was taking a deep breath and marching out onto the stage as if she performed in front of thousands every day. They were starting.

"On a cold March day in 1990," Sophie heard Kitty's voice echo from the microphone, "in the city of Belfast, Northern Ireland—"

And then Darbie was hurrying onto the stage, dressed as her ma and cradling one of Izzy's baby dolls in her arms.

The audience was quiet as Fiona, in her Mr. O'Grady overcoat and hat, swished toward Darbie while Kitty explained about his important work in "the Troubles." Kitty sounded wonderfully serious. Darbie waved to Fiona like a real wife, and Fiona hurried toward her in a husbandly way. Right on Kitty's cue, Sophie held Rory's toy gun above her head backstage and shot it. Fiona crumbled to the ground.

A scattering of chuckles came from the audience.

Sophie froze with her arm still in the air. Across the stage, Darbie looked as if she truly had been shot, before she ran, as she was supposed to, to Fiona/husband and crouched over the body until the lights dimmed and Kitty hurried off to give Fiona the script for her turn.

"They *laughed!*" she whispered as Sophie peeled the coat off Fiona. "It's the Corn Pops and the Fruit Loops."

"They're doing it on purpose, just to mess us up!" Fiona hissed.

Sophie shook her head firmly as she pushed Fiona toward the stage. "We have a mission to accomplish."

"We'll have them in tears in no time," Darbie whispered.

Fiona gave a jerk with her head and went for the microphone. Her voice rang out clear and strong. Sophie put on her Darbie hat and burst into the light.

At first, she couldn't see the faces looking up at her. In fact, it was just like being in a film with only the camera in front of her. Her camera, in Daddy's hands. She broke into a skip as Fiona told about trying to grow up in a place where other children threw rocks at her because she was Catholic. Sophie was Darbie then, and when the crumpled bags were hurled at her, she screamed as if they really were stones, and curled into a ball on the ground.

But once again the audience laughed, from way in the back. They didn't just chuckle this time. There were sure-enough Fruit Loop guffaws and Corn Pop giggles. It was only one loud "SHUSH!" from one of the adults that kept Sophie going, kept her fleeing from the "rocks" that Kitty and Darbie chased her with, disguised in their street-kid caps.

As they frantically grabbed the new set pieces and costumes backstage, Sophie could see that all the girls' eyes were wild.

"Just keep going," she said. "Just do the best you can."

She was proud of them. They did—all of them. In scene after scene they acted their hearts out, being policemen and store owners and rotten kids and the frightened Darbie and her ma. But every time a scene reached its most serious point, the back of the auditorium erupted in harsh snorts and chortles. By the time the Corn Flakes reached the part where Sophie had to kneel at Ma's graveside, she didn't have to try to cry. The tears were already choking up from the hurt place inside her. She and the Corn Flakes had tried so hard.

"It's hard for us to understand," she heard Fiona saying over the microphone, "how it was for Darbie to live with so much fear and sadness. But we have to try, because we can help her start a new life here, and we can become better people ourselves—not always acting heinous because we don't get our way, but thinking about somebody else for a change."

Sophie blinked through her tears. That last line wasn't in the script. Neither was the funny catch in Fiona's voice.

But neither were the giggles that started again in the back of the room.

It definitely wasn't in the script for Sophie to put her face in her hands and cry.

But she did.

Twelve

❋ ⌂ ✳

They didn't get it. *They didn't get it and they never will.*

The thoughts were crying out so loudly in Sophie's head she didn't realize at first that the other roar she was hearing was the audience. But they weren't laughing. They were clapping, in waves that grew stronger and stronger until they were rolling right onto the stage. Somebody was shouting, "Bravo!" and it wasn't Miss Blythe. It sounded like Daddy.

Sophie pulled her face from her hands and looked straight into the eyes of Aunt Emily and Uncle Patrick, and Kitty's mom, and Lacie. Into Daddy's camera lens and Boppa's bald head and Mama's proud face. The whole audience was standing up, and most of the ladies were wiping their eyes.

So was Dr. Peter.

"Take a bow, actors!" Miss Blythe said from the wings. "Get up—take your bows!"

Corn Flakes were suddenly grabbing Sophie from all sides and dragging her to the front of the stage where they bobbed like dashboard dogs and waved. Sophie saw Mama blowing her a kiss and Maggie standing on a chair and grinning a big square grin.

Just before they fled backstage, Sophie also saw the Corn Pops sitting with their arms folded and their eyes rolled. All except Willoughby, who whistled through her fingers until B.J. reached up and pulled her down by a handful of corkscrew curls.

"I thought the whole audience hated it when there was all that laughing!" Kitty whispered as they made their way through the dark to the backstage steps.

"That was just those Corn Pops, acting the maggot as usual," Darbie said.

Fiona grabbed Sophie by the arm and put her lips close to Sophie's ear. "You don't think it was all the parents just feeling sorry for us, do you?" she whispered.

"No," Sophie whispered back. "I think it was because of what you said. You *got* it, Fiona."

It really didn't matter then, Sophie decided, whether they won a prize or not.

Or at least, not until Miss Blythe swept up onto the stage with three envelopes in her hand. The audience went still, except for the sixth graders, who all sat on the edges of their chairs, tipping them forward and holding Miss Blythe with their eyes. Sophie's heart was slamming in her chest, and she was sure she could hear Fiona's doing the same. She thought she heard Darbie murmuring something about "Jaysus."

Even if we don't win, it's okay, Sophie prayed to him. *But we do deserve to, don't we?*

"Third prize," Miss Blythe said too loudly into the mic, "goes to . . ." She slit the envelope open with a long red fingernail. "The Karate Kids!"

The Fruit Loops whooped like monkeys on Animal Planet, and all of them scrambled up onto the stage and jumped for the envelope.

"Gentlemen," Miss Blythe said, "art is discipline."

The audience laughed one of those aren't-boys-a-mess laughs. Fiona flung her arms around Darbie, Kitty, and Sophie and whispered in a hoarse voice, "The Pops will get second prize and that's okay. We should totally clap for them."

"Of course," Sophie said. "That's what Corn Flakes do."

"We're class," Darbie said.

They squeezed each other tight, and Sophie barely noticed that Kitty was about to cut off the circulation in her left wrist. She held her breath as Miss Blythe produced the second envelope.

"Second prize goes to ..." Slice with the fingernail. Shake out the paper. "The Troubles: Darbie's Story!"

The audience shouted like one person, out-voiced only by the screams of the Corn Pops.

"That means we won!" B.J. shrieked. "We got first!"

"Can our actors come up and receive their prize?" Miss Blythe said.

There was more clapping, and somehow Sophie led the Corn Flakes up to the stage. Kitty bounced like she was on a pogo stick, and Darbie dipped her splashy hair back and forth and smiled shyly as Sophie passed the envelope to her. Her dark eyes were shimmering, and for the first time since Sophie had met her she looked like a real little girl.

But as they all bowed again, Sophie was afraid to look at Fiona. They hadn't won first prize, and it was pretty certain the Pops were going to. Fiona was facing the floor as they bowed so Sophie couldn't see it — though she was surprised Fiona didn't snatch their second prize envelope from Darbie and stomp on it.

They were barely off the stage when the audience buzzed into silence and Miss Blythe cleared her throat into the microphone. "Ladies and gentlemen," she said in a deep voice, "the first-prize winner is the Irish Showdown Dance Troupe!"

The scream Sophie expected from the Corn Pops didn't happen. Instead, while the audience clapped and whistled, they lined up in the back and cartwheeled and backflipped their way up the aisle. In front of the stage, they formed a pyramid topped by Willoughby, who leaped to the stage and started a chain to pull the rest of them up. There they struck a final pose, smiling like a toothpaste commercial.

"Do you think they thought they were going to win?" Fiona said to Sophie beneath the roar of the audience.

Sophie searched her face. Fiona was smiling and shaking her head, even as she clapped.

"Too bad they aren't class," Fiona said. She hooked her arm through Darbie's. "But we know who is."

Wow, Sophie thought. *Just — wow.*

Melting with happy relief, she latched onto Kitty with one hand and waved Maggie over with the other. The Corn Pops hadn't bothered to invite her onto the stage, and Maggie looked like she'd rather be standing with her Corn Flakes anyway. Maggie got to them just in time to smile at Daddy, who had his back turned to the stage completely and was filming Sophie and the girls with a victory grin on his face. He usually only looked like that when the Dallas Cowboys won.

There were shamrock-shaped cookies and green punch and certificates for all the participants after the show. The Corn Flakes gathered around Darbie to see what the prize in the envelope was.

"A boat tour of the Chesapeake Bay!" Darbie read.

"Just as long as somebody else is steering," Fiona said.

They grinned at each other.

Once Sophie hugged her family and Boppa and Aunt Emily, she skipped the food and went in search of Dr. Peter. He was hanging out near the punch bowl wearing his enormous green top hat.

"Sophie, me lass!" he said when he saw her. And then he dropped his Irish accent, and his eyes grew soft.

"Did you like it—was it okay?" Sophie said.

"Oh, Loodle," he said. "It was fabulous—and you know I would never lie to you. I'm so proud of you."

"I messed up a little. I wasn't supposed to cry that much at the end."

"Why not? The rest of us did." He cocked his head at her. "You weren't acting then, were you?"

"No," Sophie said. The second prize and the bravos were fizzling out of her. "I was crying because they were laughing. I guess the Corn Pops and the Fruit Loops really are that hateful."

"You think they were laughing to make you look bad?" Dr. Peter said. "It didn't work, did it?"

Sophie shook her head. She felt like she was going to cry again.

"Okay, Loodle, dish. What's going on?"

Sophie looked over her shoulder. "We're having a session right here?"

"No, this is just two friends talking about why you feel bad."

"Because our mission—it failed. We wanted everybody to understand about Darbie and how hard her life was and how there are more important things than being popular and winning and stuff. Fiona got it—right while she was up on the stage—but none of the other kids did, and they were the ones we were doing it for. They were the feet we were trying to wash." Sophie smacked at a tear with her fingers. "I just wanted them to understand."

Dr. Peter leaned down, almost covering Sophie with the brim of his hat. "I'll let you in on a little secret," he said. "I think they understood very clearly. They saw themselves up there in those kids that threw rocks and shouted mean things, and they were embarrassed. That's why they laughed."

"No offense, Dr. Peter," Sophie said. "But Corn Pops and Fruit Loops don't get embarrassed."

"Not for long, but they do have that 'oops' feeling for a bit of a moment before they cover it up. Just look over there."

Dr. Peter winked, just like a leprechaun, Sophie thought, and nodded his hat toward the stage. There were the Corn Pops, still in costume, flipping and splitting and backflipping, and completing each move with outstretched arms and a dazzling smile—like they were going for gold at the Olympics. It made Sophie feel itchy. There was performing, and then there was just plain old showing off.

For a minute Sophie thought Dr. Peter was wrong. None of them looked the least bit embarrassed about the fact that they were doing an encore that nobody was watching. Until Sophie saw a wavy-haired person slip off the front edge of the stage and look back, cheeks blotchy-red and shoulders curving almost to meet at her chest. Willoughby shook out what had survived of her bun, folded her arms across the front of her sequined top, and walked stiffly away. Behind her, the Pops gathered for a pyramid and B.J. yelled, "Hey, where's Willoughby?"

Willoughby gave a nervous laugh and disappeared into the crowd of parents.

"Embarrassed by her own kind," Dr. Peter said. "And what did she do?"

"She laughed," Sophie said. "But by Monday she'll be hanging out with them again."

"Not unless somebody else gets to her first." Dr. Peter gave her another leprechaun wink and said, "Happy St. Patty's Day, Loodle. I'll see you soon in my office. Looks like we'll have a lot to talk about."

And then with a twinkle, he was gone too.

Sophie stood there for a minute watching the Fruit Loops tearing down the streamers with karate chops and the Corn Pops showing off for no one and her own Corn Flakes introducing Darbie to their families.

There would be a lot to tell Jesus tonight when it was quiet and she could imagine him washing her feet. They were pretty tired feet. Acting was hard work.

She would tell him that she and the Flakes had shown all the love they could, maybe some to the Pops even if they didn't get it. She'd also tell him that Fiona understood finally—and Kitty—and probably Maggie. Maybe even Lacie.

And possibly somebody else who could now use a foot washing. Maybe not right away. Perhaps just an invitation to sit at their lunch table would be good first, and then a part in their upcoming film about Colleen O'Bravo.

Sophie smiled to herself. *What a class idea*, she thought.

And she went off to look for Willoughby.

Glossary

barnacled (bar-nah-KULD) when something is covered in icky sea creatures that look like little rocks or shells

bevy (bev-EE) a word used to describe the number of people that gather in one place

catastrophe (ka-tas-truh-FEE) a complete disaster, usually one that isn't easy to fix

chaperone (sha-PURR-own) an adult or person in authority who acts as a fancy babysitter

coalition (co-uh-LI-shun) a bunch of people who join together and try to change something they think is wrong

desperate (des-PER-ate) (1) When something really needs to be fixed up, or someone really needs help; (2) feeling panicked when you don't have any other choices

devastation (dev-ahs-TA-shun) when everything is falling apart and in ruins, usually because something really bad happened

diabolical (die-ah-BOLL-eh-call) a completely evil action, or at least a really terrible thing to do

disdainful (dis-DANE-full) acting like a spoiled princess and looking down on someone because you think they're acting like an idiot

guffaw (guf-FAWW) when you find something really funny, and can't help but laugh really loud

insatiably (in-SAY-shuh-blee) the state of never being completely satisfied, and always wanting to know more

nonsensical (non-SEN-si-cull) doing something so silly it defies logic

obnoxious (ob-KNOCK-shus) a person who is offensive and a complete pain in the bum, and who drives everyone crazy

pantomime (pan-TOW-mime) acting out a story without a script, using only a narrator and your body expressions to tell the story

plethora (PLETH-er-a) a general term used to describe a lot of something, like when there's almost too much

sacred (SAY-crid) something that's holy and should be treated with special care

Tasmanian devil (taz-main-E-an DEV-ill) a mean little animal that lives in Australia and looks like an overgrown rat. It's also the name of a cartoon character that has *way* too much energy.

tousled (TUH-silled) something, usually hair, that was blown about and becomes a tangled mess

usurping (you-SIRP-ing) basically, to steal something away from someone by using a lot of force to get it

Sophie and Friends

Nancy Rue

Meet Sophie LaCroix, a creative soul with a desire to become a great film director someday, and she definitely has a flair for drama! Her overactive imagination frequently lands her in trouble, but her faith and friends always save the day. This bindup includes two-books-in-one.

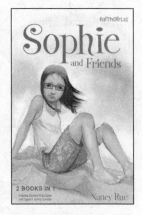

Sophie's First Dance: Sophie and her friends, the Corn Flakes, are in a tizzy over the end-of-school dance - especially when invitations start coming - from boys! Will the Flakes break up, or can Sophie direct a happy ending?

Sophie's Stormy Summer: One of the Flakes is struck with cancer, and Sophie severely struggles with the shocking news, until she finds that friends - and faith - show the way to a new adventure called growing up.

Available in stores and online!

ZONDERVAN®
.com

Sophie Flakes Out

Nancy Rue

Meet Sophie LaCroix, a creative soul with a desire to become a great film director someday, and she definitely has a flair for drama! Her overactive imagination frequently lands her in trouble, but her faith and friends always save the day. From best-selling author, Nancy Rue, comes two-in-one bindups of the popular Sophie series.

Sophie Flakes Out: Sophie wants more privacy like her friend Willoughby, who has plenty, until Willoughby's father finds out about her fast, new friends. His harsh punishment makes Sophie wonder what rules they need to follow.

Sophie Loves Jimmy: Sophie doesn't get why a rumor should stop her from being Jimmy's friend – until the Corn Flakes start believing the whispers. Now Sophie wonders how she and the Flakes can ever be friends again!

Available in stores and online!

Faithgirlz Journal

My Doodles, Dreams and Devotion

Looking for a place to dream, doodle, and record your innermost questions and secrets? You will find what you seek within the pages of the Faithgirlz Journal, which has plenty of space for you to discover who you are, explore who God is shaping you to be, or write down whatever inspires you. Each journal page has awesome quotes and powerful Bible verses to encourage you on  your walk with God! So grab a pen, colored pencils, or even a handful of markers. Whatever you write is just between you and God.

Available in stores and online!

ZONDERVAN
.com

NIV Faithgirlz! Backpack Bible, Revised Edition

Small enough to fit into a backpack or bag, this Bible can go anywhere a girl does.

Features include:

- Fun Italian Duo-Tone™ design
- Twelve full-color pages of Faithgirlz fun that helps girls learn the "Beauty of Believing!"
- Words of Christ in red
- Ribbon marker
- Complete text of the bestselling NIV translation

Available in stores and online!

Talk It Up!

Want free books?
First looks at the best new fiction?
Awesome exclusive merchandise?

We want to hear from you!

Give us your opinions on titles, covers, and stories.
Join the Z Street Team.

Email us at zstreetteam@zondervan.com
to sign up today!

Also—Friend us on Facebook!

www.facebook.com/goodteenreads

- Video Trailers
- Connect with your favorite authors
- Sneak peeks at new releases
- Giveaways
- Fun discussions
- And much more!